cat's foot

# Also by Brian Doyle

## Fiction

*Mink River*
*Bin Laden's Bald Spot*
  *and Other Stories*

## Nonfiction

*The Grail: A Year Ambling and*
  *Shambling through an Oregon*
  *Vineyard in Pursuit of the Best*
  *Pinot Noir Wine in the Whole Wild World*
*The Wet Engine: Exploring the Mad*
  *Wild Miracle of the Heart*

## Poetry

*Epiphanies and Elegies*
*Thirsty for the Joy: Australian*
  *and American Voices*

## Books of Essays

*Grace Notes*
*Leaping*
*Spirited Men*
*Saints Passionate and Peculiar*
*Credo*
*Two Voices (with Jim Doyle)*

# cat's foot

by
BRIAN DOYLE

Corby Books
Notre Dame, Indiana

CAT'S FOOT

Copyright © 2012 by Brian Doyle

ISBN 978-0-9833586-7-1

cover art by H.F. Holtgrefe

Published by
**Corby Books**
A Division of Corby Publishing LP
P.O. Box 93
Notre Dame, Indiana 46556
(574) 784-3482
www.corbypublishing.com

Manufactured in the United States of America

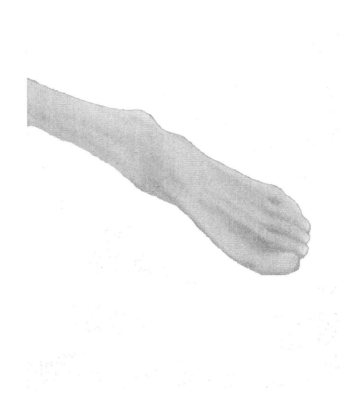

My friend Cat lost his foot in a swamp during a war. He was just walking along, he said, trying to mind his own business, when he stepped on a mine and the mine blew his foot off.

Boy, was I mad, he said. I fell down, and the guy behind me just detoured around me and kept going without even looking at me or saying anything. The guy in front of me stopped to see if he could help but when he saw my foot was missing he just shook his head and kept going. So there I was by myself in the swamp without my foot.

Well, I was the medical guy in our patrol so I cleaned the wound and stopped the bleeding as best I could and bandaged my leg up and used my rifle as a crutch and I hopped out of there, and no one shot at me, for once, and I didn't step on any more mines, so that was good.

Eventually my leg healed and the war ended and years passed, and I got to thinking about my foot. I mean, that was a good foot, and we parted so hurriedly I never had a chance to really think about it as a foot, you know what I mean? I missed my foot, is what I am trying to say. So I decided to try to find it. I asked my wife and sons if they wanted to go with me to find it but they said no thanks and I asked a couple of guys who had been in the war with me if they wanted to go but they said no thanks also so I went alone. It seemed to me that going alone was the right way anyway. It was my foot, after all, not anyone else's foot, and so it was my responsibility to go find it, not anyone else's responsibility, and if I went with anyone else, it would be an expedition or a journey or voyage something, which I didn't want it to be, I just wanted to find my foot. So I went by myself.

First I went back to the swamp, he says, but after the war the swamp had been drained and now it was a farm. I asked the farmer if I could look through the farm for my foot and he said sure. I looked and looked all over and

2

he came out after a couple days and helped me, both of us digging here and there where we thought it might be. He was a very kind man. His son was a very good student of science and he figured arcs and trajectories and detonation forces and things like that. We found a lot of bones in the fields but none of those bones were mine. Those bones had very thin shrill white voices. It's hard for me to explain. You could find them by listening if you learned how to listen. We took the bones we found and made a shed for them where they could rest until someone came for them. It took us a day to make that shed. I am proud of making that shed. No one ever thinks about sheds, that someone has to make them, and they are not so easy to make. To make a good shed you have to go slowly and build it right, first the bones and then the skin, so at least there is one more good shed in the world where there didn't used to be one. We built the shelves inside very carefully so they would never fall down and disrespect those bones. Those poor bones. Some of the bones were very old and as the son said there must have been many wars washing over this field like tides.

3

I went on, says Cat. I asked the people living nearby if they knew anything about my foot and one old woman said she saw my foot during the war after the explosion. It was in the tall grass along the road, she said, and she remembered that it had a red sock and a black boot.

O, yes, that was my foot, I said.

Did the sock have little black birds on it also? she asked.

Yes, I said, those were tiny crows, my gramma made those socks for me, she and I loved crows and she stitched tiny crows onto the socks so I would remember her sometimes during the war. We used to go listening for crows where we lived, I told the old woman. We would walk for miles and miles. There were sure a lot of crows where we lived. We would make crow sounds and the crows would talk back to us. If you listen you can hear a lot of songs that animals sing, my gramma would say. Crows mostly sing rude songs, some of them would make you blush.

That is so, said the old woman. Here it is more the cranes and owls that talk back to you. I talk to the cranes during the day and the owls at night. Some of those owls used to be

4

people, you know, long ago, but the war took them and they returned to this place as night birds. That's what happens to some people. God puts them back here in another form. Maybe so they don't die in wars. You never see owls dying in wars.

Did some of the cranes used to be people too? I ask.

No, no, says the old woman. Silly talk. Cranes are always cranes.

The old woman said that my foot was pointing south when she saw it, so I went south. I traveled for a long time. Sometimes by bicycle and sometimes walking. Every day I would ask people if they had ever seen my foot and every day someone would say yes and point, so I went where they pointed. I went for many miles and many days. I had not been back in this place since the war and at that time I didn't see much of the countryside, to be honest, so this was new country to me.

One day my leg hurt me greatly and I was resting by the side of the road when a man came by on his bicycle. I said hello and he said hello and he asked where was my foot. I told him it was in this country somewhere and I was looking for it and he said perhaps I should have another foot until that happened. I told him that I had tried artificial feet after the war but they were very uncomfortable and I had gotten along with my stick.

Ah, but I make all sorts of things, he said. I am a woodworker. Allow me, sir.

He examined my leg for a while and said he thought he could make me three new feet in the course of a day, and if I did not have any immediately pressing plans perhaps I could rest a day in his village while he made the feet, and then I could be on my way. I pointed out that I had very little money but he said prayers for children would be sufficient so I agreed and he gave me a ride to the village on his bicycle.

The village was filled with dogs and chickens and children and the little houses smelled like cinnamon. At the woodworker's house I sat on the porch and told stories to his children while he made me a new foot. There were two children, both girls and both very small, and I told them stories about animals and boats. I told them stories about cougars and coyotes, bobcats and seals, falcons and eagles, and about the boat I had as a boy, and the boats that had ferried me across oceans, and boats that could fly, and boats that could swim underwater.

The woodworker made a bamboo foot first, as bamboo grew everywhere around us and was easy to work with, but that bamboo wouldn't carry much weight and the foot splintered after I took two steps. Then he made three wooden feet, one from red wood, and one from black wood, and one from gray wood, but while all of them bore weight gracefully none was very comfortable, so finally he made a foot from rubber, and this was a most excellent foot, bearing weight beautifully but also providing bounce and resilience, not to mention traction. We were both delighted, he that he had arrived at the right foot on the fifth try, and me to have a new foot after many years. It was like having a hand on the end of your arm again after many years! Imagine that!

The rubber, said the woodworker, came from a tire left over from the war. There were a lot of tires and pieces of metal left after the war, and also bombs and mines that never got their chance to explode during the war. You *almost* felt bad for those bombs and mines, he said, that never got to do what they were born to do. Every once in a while someone in the village stepped on a mine in the woods and he or she vanished or was found later, missing a part. Curiously this never happened to animals. So when people say the war is over, said the woodworker, I say, well, the war is not all the *way* over, and it might not be all the way over for a very long time. Wars are not events as much as they are diseases to be recovered from with lots of scars, or conditions with which to grapple for centuries, or a set of circumstances that have to be figured out very slowly, each solution giving birth to new problems. Perhaps wars end in reverse proportion to how quickly they began. Or perhaps they never actually end at all, just change form.

I don't think I can easily explain how great it was to have a foot again, said Cat, even if it was a foot made of rubber from a truck tire. I kept my stick, of course, because a good stick is a good friend, and you don't throw away good friends. But to be able to walk more quickly, and to walk in balance, was a most remarkable feeling. I no longer listed to starboard, for one thing, and everything seemed fresh and new to me, arranged in different proportions, the horizon horizontal, trees elegantly vertical, everything speaking a new geometrical language. A most remarkable feeling. You know the feeling you have after you have been ill for weeks, and you finally are well enough to leave your bed, and step outside into the green riot of the world, and you gasp at the color and music of it all, and feel like you have been issued new eyes and ears? I felt like that with my whole body. Most remarkable.

The woodworker took the four discarded wooden feet and added short stilts to them and gave them to his little girls and they instantly balanced on them and stalked off hilarious. Do you remember the foot you used to have? the woodworker asked. Not so well, I said. I suppose it was very like this other foot, all sinew and tiny bones and startling toes, but I was only twenty years old when we parted company, and many years have passed. I didn't consider my feet at all when I was young, only when they were injured. I took them for granted. We take everything for granted. Perhaps we must, otherwise we would do nothing but sit around amazed at all the miracles, and nothing would ever get done, no laundry, no cooking, no making stilts for little girls.

I borrowed some sheets of paper, says Cat, and I wrote down some of the stories I had told the little girls about animals, and they folded them up into tiny squares and put them in tiny wooden boxes. The woodworker wouldn't accept any money for making me feet but I slipped coins into the girls' pockets and whispered that the coins were magic and they should wait one whole day and then produce them magically from their pockets to show their father and he would be most amazed and astonished. Then I went on.

Now I was in a country of rivers, says Cat, and they were everywhere braided and woven, tiny creeks and streams and rivulets, some silver and some green and some sluggish and brown and looking like enormous snakes. I walked for hours that day just happy to have a new foot. It had been many years since I could say even the words *I walked for hours*, and I spent that day inside those four words, you might say. Every day has a flavor, when you think about it. Some days are talking days, some days are laughing days, some days are loving, some are angry, some are praying days, some are days of the body. You know what I mean. It isn't what you **do** that day that's

10

the theme of the day, it's what you *felt*, does that make sense? And what I remember of that day is the feel of moving steadily briskly along the road, swinging my stick. I should remember if it was hot or cool, and what that country smelled like, and the colors of trees and houses and people in the fields, and the music of birds, and if I was hungry or thirsty, but all I remember is that I was so very happy to be walking that I thought I was going to float away up into the air.

I came to a town, says Cat, and I stopped there to eat, and within a few minutes a police-man appeared and asked me questions very politely. I answered him as best I could, ex-plaining that I had returned to the country to find my foot, which I had lost in the war, and he examined my papers carefully, and thanked me and went away. I got a second cup of tea, and just as I was finishing it and ready to get back to walking, two soldiers appeared and sat down at the table.

They were very polite also, but they were most curious about which army I had been in during the war, and where I had been then and since then, and where I intended to go now. I told them about my service, and said that I had no particular specified destination as yet, and

13

was engaged in a general search, and after listening quietly they asked me to accompany them to their headquarters, where there were any number of other conversations to be had, as the younger soldier said politely. He seemed very young, perhaps not yet twenty, the sort of young man in whom you can still see the essence of boy.

There is a quiet respect, almost a camaraderie, among soldiers of whatever armies are not in direct opposition, you know, soldiers tend to respect each other, so I went with them to their headquarters.

There they asked me to wait in a quiet wooden room with a table and two chairs. It was very hot. After a few moments an older man came in and sat down. He was perhaps my age, a man of military bearing. He said that he was the chief of the soldiers in this district and that part of his job was to be aware of any people he was not aware of, which is why he was going to ask me questions, and he would be most grateful if I would answer them forthrightly.

You were in the army, he said.

Yes.

The other army.

It was the only one I could join when I was young, I said.

It was the wrong army.

Perhaps.

Our army was victorious.

Yes.

So you are an enemy.

Not anymore, I said.

You fled the country after our forces were victorious.

I prefer to say that I emigrated at a time when prospects for me seemed dim.

You had permission to leave?

I didn't think I was the sort of citizen who would be missed.

So you left without permission, robbing the nation of a crucial resource, and evading responsibility for your crimes during the revolution of the people.

No, I said. I served in the army of the land in which I was born, a land that was defeated by the army of another land, an army that then occupied the land where my ancestors have lived for thousands of years. Having served honorably, and sustained wounds, I found myself unemployable and in constant danger of imprisonment or worse under the new authority. As every man does, I wished for peace, for a land where I could perhaps marry and be granted children, a land where I could work and care for my family, a land where who I had once been was no longer my definition. Of my own volition I decided to leave this land. I say to you as one soldier to another, we fought against each other long ago, but that time is past, and now is the time to respect each other, not to apportion blame.

But crime must be punished, said the chief.

If your army had lost the war, would you be a criminal now?

But we did not lose.

You might have.

We knew we would win.

But what if you hadn't?

This is treasonous talk. Our army won because we were destined to win. Your army lost because you were in the wrong. That was proven.

And now the army in which I served is long dissolved, its surviving soldiers returned to fields and cities. Or traveling, as I am.

Your traveling is now finished. In the name of the state I arrest you for crimes against the people, and for evading the punishment due to war criminals.

I remember that moment so vividly, said Cat. It was very hot in the room, and the chief had never raised his voice, but simply spoke that sentence in a murmur, as if he was remarking upon the weather. For a couple of minutes neither of us said anything and then the door opened and the same two soldiers came in. The very young soldier gently took my stick away and the older soldier gave me his shoulder to lean on as they accompanied me to my cell. There didn't seem to be anything to say so no one said anything. I remember the murmur of rain.

My cell was down the stairs and under the ground. There were five cells down there and men in three of the cells. The cells were small and each one had a sliver of window about five inches high and eighteen inches long. There was a cot and a pot. The older soldier knelt down and gently took my new foot off. He said that he was very sorry to remove my foot but the chief had ordered him to do so. The younger soldier stood by the door and didn't say anything. They gave me a pitcher of water and a blanket. The older soldier said that I might as well try to get some sleep, so I did.

The two other men in cells were down at the other end of the row. One man was quite old, it seemed to me, and he was silent. The other man was younger but appeared quite sick, and he spoke a language I didn't know. He said something to me in his language and I gestured that I didn't understand and he subsided.

The afternoon and the evening passed. I thought about my wife and sons. That's what I do when I have time to just sit and think. I just think about them slowly. I think about their faces, and then their voices, and then their bodies, and then adventures they have had, and their favorite foods, and how they danced, and laughed, and cried, and how they look in the bed when they are sleeping. My wife curls up in a little ball when she sleeps, but one of my boys sleeps all over the bed, you know, one leg here and one leg there, his arms flung out any old way, but his brother is the other way around, whatever way he falls asleep is how he sleeps all the rest of the night. That boy can fall asleep anywhere anyhow. He used to sleep on my shoulder all the time when he was little.

I thought the chief or the soldiers or a policeman or someone would come and talk to me before the night came, that first night in the jail, says Cat, but no one did, so I fell asleep. But in the morning the chief came, by himself, with a long stick like a whip, and I got a bad feeling. Things like this had happened to me long ago.

You carried weapons against us, said the chief.

I served honorably.

You murdered citizens.

I fought for the land of my ancestors.

Your first crime was to bear arms against us, he said, and he lashed me.

The rest of the morning was like that, says Cat. He would ask me questions, and I would answer them, and then he would lash me. It was pointless to struggle or try to evade the lash. That first morning the two soldiers were there in case I struggled but I didn't. Every day it was like that, he would question me and lash me in the morning and the rest of the day I spent in my cell.

19

I lost hope a little on the fourth day, says Cat, and the next morning I lost my temper while being lashed, and the chief lost his temper, and he lashed me so hard there was blood on the floor. The two soldiers carried me back to my cell and gave me water. That night when I was sleeping the younger soldier came and silently let me out of my cell and gave me my foot back, and my stick, and told me to walk in the river a few hundred yards and then borrow whatever bicycle I could find and bicycle as hard as I could into the forest. We'll never find you if you go deep enough into the forest, and leave no indication of your direction, he said. You go south and we will endeavor to search in the other direction. Remember you are bleeding so you have to walk in the river for a while. I am sorry for what happened here. Prayers on your children. Go.

I did what he said, says Cat, and by morning I was quite deep in the forest. When I was a child my uncle showed me how to find great hollow trees to hide in. If you follow where the bees fly to, you can often find trees like that, so I found one and spent the day in it, sleeping. It was a bee tree but the bees were way up at the top and we didn't bother each other. Some honey had slid down inside the tree and I ate that. It was most delicious. Bees are another thing no one says thank you enough for. I really like and admire bees. They just do their work and don't bother anyone unless you bother them and then they are your enemies as long as it takes to teach you to leave them alone. They are most remarkable creatures.

I went on, says Cat. Pretty soon I got a ride from a man on a motorcycle. He was carrying chickens in a tremendous basket that wrapped all the way around the whole back of his motorcycle. You wouldn't believe there would be room for him and me and a hundred chickens but there was. It was a most remarkable motorcycle. The chickens were alive and they were *not* happy about being crammed in the basket. They were complaining as loud as I have ever heard chickens complain. They would have made a tremendous racket but they were crammed in so tightly I don't think any of them could quite get a whole lungful of air to really cut loose, so the sound was more a really loud murmuring than squawking or screeching or shrieking or burbling or any of the other words we use for chicken talk.

The man on the motorcycle was the chicken man for the local villages, he said, a position of some importance, as people there ate little meat and the fish they used to eat were no longer in the rivers, in fact fish and meat had become badges of importance and money, status symbols, foods you would serve to show off to an esteemed guest, or serve at your daughter's wedding. The country had become very poor since the war, he said, poorer than it looked, because while it looked verdant and orderly, the fields and orchards like a chess board, the river sliding gently through the scene like a painting, the reality was that most of the produce went to the government, in one way or another. It was peaceful, yes, he said, and peace was a great thing, no one would ever wish not to have peace, so that was good.

He took me to his house, in which he lived with his granddaughter, his wife and children having died in the war. His granddaughter was perhaps twenty years old, a quiet dark person who shook my hand politely and then vanished.

24

She doesn't talk very much, said the chicken man. A sweet and wonderful girl, but quiet. She was born the day after the war ended. Her mother, my daughter in law, disappeared a week later. To this day we are not sure what happened to her. Some people say she is living in the mountains but I don't think so. A lot of people just vanished. One of the things no one says about wars when they end is that a lot of people are wounded in ways you can't see. You lost a foot, and I think my lost daughter in law lost the parts of her that were attached to people. Some people say she went to the city and sells herself, but I don't think that's so. I have been to the city twice and I didn't see her. Would you like some tea? Where did you get your stick?

This reminds me I should tell you about my stick, says Cat. A most remarkable stick altogether. My father cut it for me when I was about to go to the war. A war is a different country, he said, and I would need a good stick in that new country, for all sorts of reasons that would become clear to me the deeper into it I went. This turned out to be true. My father had been in a war too, you see, and he knew what he was talking about. His father had also been

25

in a war. Perhaps all of the men in my family have been in wars all the way back to when we began. Perhaps all men ever have been in wars. Perhaps men are the reasons for wars and if there weren't any men there wouldn't be any wars, although if there weren't men soon there wouldn't be any women either, yes?

One of the things I wish most is that my sons never have to be in any wars, although I cannot see where that can happen. But you never know. They are young yet. Sometimes I have thought of making good sticks for them to have in case they have to go to wars, but for some reason I refrain. I think it is a father's fear. Fathers are filled with fears, you know. You are a father and you know that. But we never talk about our fears very much. Perhaps we should talk about them more. Perhaps if we talked about them more they would shrivel or we would use more of our brains to make them go away. I don't know.

The problem with me telling you stories like this, says Cat, is that you're not *there* in the story, you can't smell the smell of the swamp, or hear the hissing voice of the chief of the soldiers, or see the amazing way the chicken man crammed all those chickens into a basket on his motorcycle. It would be better if you could smell and hear things when I told them. But I suppose we will have to do the best we can.

We were talking about my stick, says Cat. What a wonderful stick it is. It is very strong, and has survived much use, and is as strong now as it was when it was young. It is balanced exactly right, do you know what I mean, you could rest it on one finger and hold it in the air and it would feel light and easy although it is as strong as a bone. I am not sure what kind of wood it is, my father never told me that, but it is very dark and now after the years it is shiny. My father rubbed it and rubbed it with bone, and rubbed it and rubbed it with oils, and he played music over it and said prayers over it, and submerged it in a river for a night, and when he handed it to me I could see that he was very proud of his work, which made me happy, you know that feeling of sensing that your dad is happy, and that makes you happy? Because so often a dad is distracted and worried about things.

One friend of mine said to me once that I should mount my stick over the fireplace like a trophy or something, it had traveled so far and seen so many adventures and was such a remarkable stick, but I said no no, that stick is a working stick, it wouldn't be happy to be in a shrine or be like a picture you just look at. No no. Silly talk. That stick is happiest out on the road. It wants to be in my hand, you can tell. I lean it against the front door at home, by everyone's shoes. I think the shoes and the stick like each other. They are all working for the family, of course.

Sometimes I think my stick helped people help me, says Cat. They would see me walking along with my stick, and see that I was a walking man, a traveler, not out for anything, nothing else in my hand, no gun or bill or petition or thing to sell, and they would feel a little warmer toward me maybe, as if I was doing something they would like to do, perhaps. And everyone walks, of course. And everyone has been on journeys where they need help from people, yes?

It is still the custom of the country there for travelers to be welcomed where practicable, says Cat, and you would be surprised how often I was invited to share a meal, even among people who hardly had enough themselves, or given a place to sleep, even among people who had little in the way of sturdy shelter. Once I remember being given fruit by a family who, I was sure, had nothing themselves to eat; and more than once I was given a bed by someone who then slept on the floor beside me; and once a man gave me his cot and then went and slept in his barn. These are the kind of things I remember best, the little gestures that were of course not little at all, the kindnesses that arose unbidden and for which I could not pay. All I could offer in return was gratitude and prayer at the time, and memory since; for memory is of course a form of prayer, don't you think so?

I did receive one package from home while I was gone, says Cat. It was a box with two pairs of socks, photographs of my wife and sons and dog, and drawings of little things around the house and yard by the boys. There was a note from the boys that they had taken a whole morning and went around drawing plants and bushes and the tool shed and the doors and windows. Milk bottles, coffee cups, forks and spoons, berries, the way the newspaper was flopped open on the couch. The toaster, from several different angles. Pillows and blankets and slippers under the

29

bed. Homework papers. The door to the garage, which doesn't close all the way. Pitchforks and shovels and clipper we use for the hedges. One son crawled under my truck and drew what it looked like from underneath. Also in the package was a handkerchief that smelled like my wife does when she comes out of the bath in the morning and applies oils and powders. Also there was a very old tennis ball with a note that it was a present from our dog. Also there were hair clippings from one of my sons that he saved after a haircut. Also there was a sports section from the newspaper with all the baseball box scores, some of them highlighted with tiny exclamation points next to them. Also there were candy bars and a bill from the electric company on which one of my sons wrote *I paid this for you, dad*.

Well, I was telling you about the chicken man, says Cat. A most remarkable man. He offered to take me with him on his motorcycle around the villages, so I could ask people about my foot, and we did this, and I enjoyed his company. He was a gentle and thoughtful man. His great worry was his granddaughter, because she didn't talk very much, and so access to her heart was hard to come by, because you couldn't easily tell what she was thinking, so he didn't know if she was lonely, which was his greatest worry. It wasn't that he wanted to marry her off or see her married at all, necessarily. It was just that he was an older fellow and a chicken man, and she was so quiet he didn't know if she wanted to be a teacher or fly airplanes or be a nun or what.

Maybe she wants to sell chickens, I said.

That could be, he said. Certainly she knows a great deal about chickens.

Does she like them?

Well, how can you not like them? he said. Chickens are wonderful to eat, they are easy to handle, the eggs are delicious, and really the only thing you have to watch out for is hawks. A hawk will do anything to get a chicken. I think the idea for helicopters came from somebody who watched a hawk hang in the air over a chicken pen. I have seen hawks fly through tiny holes to get chickens, snatch chickens from my motorcycle, and other things like that. You wonder who the first hawk that caught a chicken was, long ago, and what he said to the other hawks when he got home, he probably said something like *boys, everything's different, starting today.*

Anyway, says Cat, that chicken man took me all over that part of the country, and I talked to a lot of people who remembered the time right after the war when there were a lot of bones still lying everywhere, and most people were pretty sure that south was still the right direction, so I continued on south. I had a fine last dinner with the chicken man and his granddaughter, eggs and fruit and vegetables and a very salty bread she made that was really delicious. I asked her about what she wanted to do for her work but she just smiled and didn't say anything. She gave me so much bread to carry in my pockets when I went on that I waddled when I walked and she and her grandfather were almost falling down laughing. You should have seen them laughing, they had to hold onto each other so as not to fall down, you know how people do that sometimes?

# IV

I went on, says Cat, south, toward the mountains. There began to be a lot of rain. Let me
tell you about the things I smelled and saw
and tasted and touched and heard while I
was walking. First of all there was the rain.
That rain came from every direction, including
sometimes up from the ground, so that your
feet would get wetter than your head. True
thing. It was rain you could touch, rain so thick
and dense sometimes that it was the color
of metal. Gray and blue and silver, like a rifle
barrel. Rain that drummed and hammered,
rain that fell so hard in one spot that you could
be standing with one hand in the rain and the
other hand dry as dust. That happened to me.

And every kind of mud you could ever
imagine. Sucking mud and slippery mud and

mud that dried so thick and firm on your shoes that you had to knock it off with a stone and it made a loud noise when it hit the ground like a stone. And dust that sometimes would be eight inches think so you would be shuffling and plowing through it like sand. There was so much dust there! You always had dust in your hair and teeth and eyes and food and everywhere else too!

In the forest everything was wet and you could smell things dying and being born and dying again. A loud green rough smell. That forest had been there for thousands of years. It had been there long before there were any people. It knew that and you knew that. There wasn't much room in it for people, really. People were a kind of animal that didn't fit there anymore. That's why people cut it down as much as they did, you know? It was a sort of war between people and the forest. It was amazing to me how fast the forest took back land it had lost in the war. In the forest there were bomb craters that now were ponds thick with plants and fish and insects.

There were spiders the size of plates there and butterflies and birds every color you could ever imagine. There were insects of every shape and size. Sometimes I thought the country was an ocean of insects on which there were boats called people and trees and houses and so forth. There were monkeys and deer and wild pigs and small bears way up in the mountains. Some people said there were still tigers. Everybody had a story about a tiger taking a child or a dog from a village. At night you would hear lizards and crickets. You could tell if someone was walking toward you in the forest if the lizards and crickets went quiet. I never could stop being fearful when that happened. I think the war is still in me, and I only feel it again when something like that happens. When I was in the forest at night and the lizards and crickets went quiet I would crouch low and get my stick ready and prepare to fight. The first time that happened to me I realized that my body was ready to fight before my mind was. True thing. Maybe that is the problem with human beings still, is that our minds are not in charge of our bodies yet, and our bodies are still afraid of what is coming through the forest at night.

There were also a lot of funny moments, I should say that, says Cat, I have been telling this story like it is all serious and a voyage or a journey or or something but it wasn't like that, it was just me walking along trying to find my foot, that's all, and there were a lot of silly things, and times when I was sick, and times when I thought I was an idiot and a fool, and times when I cried because I missed my wife and sons so much, and maybe I would have an accident and never see them again.

But I was talking about funny moments. Here is one. One time I was walking along and an old woman stopped me because she was convinced I was a priest and she needed a priest in the *worst* way, she said. She made me come and sit down in a park on a bench and hear her confession, which she said was terribly overdue. I tried to explain that I was not a priest but she insisted that I *was* a priest, she could tell, and she started to get upset at me saying that I wasn't, so I said I would be *honored* to hear what she had to say, and she started talking, and I bet I was on that bench for three hours. She sure had a blizzard of sins to confess. You wouldn't think an old lady would be have had the time and energy to commit such a thicket of sins but she sure had put her time to good use, I can say that. It was a wonder, the life she had had. I promised her that her blizzard of sins would be safe with me, even though I was not a priest, and she said whatever my reasons were for hiding my priesthood were okay with her, she was not going to ask questions, she was the last person on earth to think ill of anyone else for reasons I could now understand, and then she gave me some food and I went on. *That* was a memorable day.

And there were many moments of fear and danger, I should say that too, says Cat. One time I was chased by a robber and it was all I could do to evade his grasp. This was in a small city and I ran and ran until he stopped running behind me. Which was a good thing because I had hurt my leg while running, my new foot had twisted and the muscle in my calf was all twisted and knotted or something, but I didn't stop running until the robber stopped, and then boy, did my leg hurt! Although later I had to laugh a little, realizing that it had been years and years since I had hurt that leg running, and realizing too that I couldn't sprain that ankle ever again, that's for sure, because there was no ankle! Ha!

And I did run out of money completely

a couple of times, and spend a day or two without eating, says Cat, but one thing the war and the years after the war had taught me was how to get by without eating for a day or two, you just drink a lot of water, or if you are really really hungry you suck on a pebble. I was taught that trick by a man in my patrol, who had learned it from his grandfather, who had been in a famine. Another thing I learned in the war was to always keep some crusts of bread in my pocket, because if you are hungry and there's nothing to eat you break off a little piece of hard crust and just suck on that for a while, and that helps.

And of course I got sick here and there, says Cat, and that was the worst, because when you are sick you get closest to losing hope. It has something to do with energy. When I was sick I would cry for my sons and my wife. I would cry thinking that maybe I would never feel their hands on my face again and their arms around me pressing me. You would think that I would think about my wife's beautiful kisses and the way her body smells like honey and salt when we are naked together, but no, it was her hand on my face that I thought about, and the way my sons

38

put their hands on my shoulders, and held my hands with their fingers when they were little, those were the things that I cried about. Remarkable.

I don't talk so much about going to find my foot, says Cat, because most people start asking sensible questions after a while and I can't answer them. Like they ask, how long were you gone? and how did you know where to go? and how much did it cost? and weren't you scared? and was this some kind of an emotional crisis thing? and did you really and truly expect to find a foot that had been blown off years and years ago? Questions like that, for which I had no answers. Well, I could answer the last one. Yes, I did expect to find my foot. Otherwise why would I go?

But you are not asking me those kind of questions, says Cat. You are an unusual person. And I am not asking *you* any kind of questions. Perhaps we should do this the other way around, and I ask you questions, and you tell me stories, and I write them down. No? Why do you laugh? Don't you have a lot of stories to tell? I bet you do. Everyone does, of course. It's just that not enough people ask other people to tell their stories, and the people who don't get asked get shy about telling their stories. I think this is the reason people get married and have children in the end. It's so you'll have more stories. That's why people live in towns and cities too. More stories. Although there are a lot of stories in the woods and fields. But animal stories are different kinds of stories, and you can't just hear those kinds of stories if you are a person, you need person stories. Stories are like food, you can't just eat one kind, you have to eat different kinds to be healthy. That's one thing I know.

I know a lot about heating, ventilation, and air conditioning, says Cat, and about valves and ducts, and something of electricity and its behaviors, and engineering, and a little carpentry. Other than that I don't know much. A little about my wife and sons, but they are different all the time, and whatever you think you know about people, you don't know for long, isn't that right? Also I know a little about birds and animals, but I feel that everyone knows a little about birds and animals, how could you not, they are all around, and you learn things about them just by being alive, yes? You would have to be blind deaf dumb and willfully ignorant not to know anything about all the other beings who live here on this particular planet.

One thing that has been very useful for me to know, concludes Cat, is engines and motors. You wouldn't believe how useful a little basic mechanical skill is, and anyone can learn it. I don't have any patience with people who say they are clumsy or bookish and cannot learn basic mechanical skills. Silly talk. Just take your time and you can figure it out, that's the rule for fixing things. That should be the rule for everything, yes? Science people are always talking about the one law that binds the universe, the law of laws, but it's right there in front of our eyes, *slow down!* That's the first rule of the universe!

# V

One day, says Cat, I saw a religion being born, did I tell you that story? I was walking along through the fields and in the distance there was a tall young tree with a lot of people sitting around it. They were humming or singing gently or maybe praying. I went there and sat down. They were very welcoming, those people. There might have been two hundred people of all ages including what seemed to be a lot of babies. It turned out the tree had just sprouted on the spot where a young woman had vanished, just disappeared into the air, two teenagers had witnessed the young woman evanescing, and very soon after a tree grew on the spot, and the unusual thing was that the tree wasn't native there, no one knew what kind of tree it was, no one had ever seen that kind of tree before, and people began to come and touch it for luck, and sit near it to think and consider, and pretty soon there were people coming from miles around to touch the bark, and sit in the shadow it cast, because its shade was considered beneficial and merciful, and people told stories of good things happening after they touched the tree or spoke to it or sat in its shade. I sat there listening to their stories for a long time. They were most remarkable stories. There were all sorts of stories about the young woman, no one seemed to know exactly who she was, or she had been a lot of different people, perhaps, because there were all sorts of stories, more than you would think would gather around a woman so young, but I didn't say anything, I just listened.

Another day, says Cat, I saw children all day long, I mean really *saw* them, for a change. We notice them but we don't *see* them, you know what I mean? It started that day with a boy in a wagon, he had no legs, he was just scooting along using his arms, but the wagon was painted the brightest most startling happiest orange you ever saw, and that boy was so happy, it was a most remarkable thing. Well, after I saw that boy, my eyes opened wider, and I saw so many stunning children I often had to sit down and take a breath. Little girls holding hands, and a boy with a mouse in a string, and a boy in a tree looking down at me like an owl, and a boy selling bolts of cloth the color of stars, and a girl with clouds in her eyes, and a boy wearing a crown like a tiny king, and one time a parade of the smallest children along the road, perhaps they were coming from or going to school, they were running along, each one holding the shirt-tail of the one in front. A most remarkable sight.

That boy with the mouse on a string, I talked to him for a while, and he and the mouse were very close. They had had a tremendous number of adventures. They had known each other for years, since they were very little, and each had helped the other through innumerable scrapes and escapes. One time a cat was chasing the mouse and almost caught him when the boy threw a lizard all the way across the yard and the lizard went right in the cat's ear! Ha! What a tremendous throw! Although the boy said right away he didn't do it on purpose. But remarkable things happen sometimes. Another time the boy was about to trip a wire in the forest that was attached to land mines still from the war and the mouse shouted and the boy stopped dead in his tracks for a moment until he noticed the silvery thread. Another time the mouse jumped on a snake and went for the ride of its life, you bet, the snake trying to whip around and eat it and the mouse hanging on like a man on a horse, ha! There were a lot of other adventures they had, that boy and that mouse. I will have to try to remember them for you. Ask me again sometime.

Another time, says Cat, I stumbled across a building filled to the rafters with weapons. You wouldn't believe how many weapons there were and how many kinds of weapons there were. It was like a museum of weapons. Rifles and machine-guns and shotguns and carbines and automatic guns, yes, but also crossbows, and all sorts of knives and spears and lances, and even halberds and bows and arrows. They were all just piled in vast piles everywhere, and it was a huge building. Nothing was in order or boxed or anything like that. It was as if several armies had been disarmed at the same time and all their weapons were stored away and

46

that was that. There was no one there. Most remarkable. It seemed rather a haunted place so I walked away from there as quickly as I could.

Then there came a day when I *did* see the chief of soldiers again, says Cat. It was night and I was walking through the edge of the forest, along a line of hills. I had seen soldiers on the road and it seemed like a good idea to walk inside the forest. I heard voices ahead of me and a truck went by with soldiers who didn't see me. I was very cautious and stayed in the shadows. One thing you learn while walking at night is that there are dark places and then darker places. Deep pools of dark. Well, I was standing in one of these pools, close to the line of hills, and suddenly a man lit a cigarette, not ten feet away, and it was the chief of soldiers!

Something came over me, a feeling I hadn't felt in many years, and I regret to say that instead of slipping away as a sensible man would have done, I slipped up behind him and grabbed him by the neck and threw him to the ground and sat on him with my stick against his neck. His eyes bulged and he tried to yell and throw me off but I pressed my stick against his neck so hard he could hardly breathe.

I had noticed a cave near by, a place I thought I might sleep that night, and I took the chief's gun away and made him walk there.

You were in the wrong army, I said. Your army killed a lot of my friends. Your army killed a lot of people who never did anything to you. Your army became a government that steals from everybody. Your army ended up being a worse government than the government that you rebelled against.

You don't live here anymore, said the chief, so why should I listen to you?

Because this time I have the weapon and you are the prisoner, I said, and I lashed him across the legs with my stick.

I am sorry to admit that I did that, says Cat very quietly. I regret my action. I have no explanation or excuse. That is what I did.

We were in the cave all night long, says Cat, and there were three times that I remember that I almost killed that man. Once he tried to rush past me and I grabbed his throat. Once he began to yell and I grabbed his throat again. And once he admitted that he killed a man in my army by beating him to death, and I lost my temper and raised my stick to beat him right into the floor of the cave but somehow I didn't. Something stopped me. Maybe I stopped me. I wish I could say I had a vision of my children, or that a holy person spoke inside my brain, or that my wife's face appeared in front of my eyes and lifted the violence from my hand, but none of that happened. I just stopped. I don't know why. It is a mystery.

I ended up tying him with a rope and leaving the cave myself, says Cat. It seemed like the thing to do. He would be found soon enough, people would look for him, and if I left in the dark then no one would know where I went. So I did that. I talked to him a while before I left, and tried to explain that I wasn't in a war anymore, and didn't want to fight with him, but I can't say that he was receptive to what I was trying to say, so I left. Sometimes you just have to close up the shop and walk on, so that's what I did.

People say to me, what about God, says Cat, and I say what about God? You cannot tell me that God had anything to do with me and the chief of soldiers, or with my foot being blown off, or with what happened in the war. God has nothing to do with it. God allowed living things, and then what happens to the living things happens to them, that's up to them. Wars are our fault. Poor God, I think. God has to sit and watch feet being blown off and worse. God must want to put his stick against our throat sometimes and say enough! But that doesn't happen, which makes me think God sure loves living things. People say no, that means there is no God, or God is remote, but that's silly thinking. If God was interrupting all the time, what kind of the life would that be? Not much. It would be like God was the chief of soldiers for everyone, telling everyone what to do. No. God is not like that. I don't know what God is like, but I know what God *isn't* like! Ha!

# VI

Did I ever tell you, says Cat, what happened to me right after the war? No?

Well, there I was, missing a foot, a veteran of the wrong army, and prospects looked dim. So I concluded to escape. But I didn't have any money. My sister, however, agreed with me that I should escape, so she found money somehow, and I found a man who would lead me across the border. An *excellent* sister. I wish I saw more of her but she lives very far away now and has five children.

We walked through the forest, this man and I, and then we went through the mountains in his wagon. The mountains went on and on like the tide in the sea. I had never seen so many mountains or such a dense forest. I had spent all my years to that point in the city, in the lowlands, and the mountains to me as a child were only a rumor. You would see them in books or hear about them in stories. Well, up we went through the mountains, the man with the wagon and me, and whenever he thought we were coming to a place where there might be people he made me get under the load in the wagon, which was bags and bags of vegetables, and they were really heavy! You wouldn't believe how hard it is to lie there under a thousand pounds of vegetables! But finally he delivered me to the border. The way you could tell it was the border was that the government mowed a line right through the forest, about ten yards wide, with tractors and bulldozers and trucks, and there were teams of men whose job it was to keep the line clear, they started at one end of the line and worked along cutting bushes and uprooting the little trees, and by the time they got to the end enough time would have passed that they would drive back to the start and do it over again.

So I had to get across that line in the dark, says Cat, and there were soldiers around in the forest, you could never tell where they were, so I waited on my side of the line until it was really dark, and then a bunch of people all ran across the line at once. It was so dark I could hardly see, and I couldn't run too well, of course, without my foot, but one of the people ahead of me had a white shirt and I followed that man as fast as I could go. People say how did you run across the border? and I say I didn't run, I hopped really fast! Ha!

Did I ever tell you, says Cat, about those other guys who were in my patrol in the war? The guys who detoured around me after my foot blew off in the swamp? No?

Well, one man, we called him the Stork because he was so tall, he became a school-teacher, and still is. Another man we called Monkey Man, he died. Another man who was our captain, he died. Another man, Laughing Man, he became the mayor of a town and he has eleven children and has a factory that makes shoes. Another man went to the city after the war and no one ever heard of him again. Another man went into the forest near the border and no one ever heard of him again. Another man became an engineer in another country. There were two other men I don't know what happened to them. You just get put together in a war and you do the best you can to get along. There were ten of us. People say your fellow soldiers become closer than brothers but that didn't happen to me. It was like they were teammates on a soccer team, that's what it was like. You have to work together but you don't have to like each other all that much. I liked the Stork. He was a very funny and he would share his food, that sort of guy. I bet he became a very good teacher. He liked children and they liked him, that sort of guy. He would have stopped to help me when my foot was lost in the swamp but he was first man in line that day and he never knew it was me who was left behind. He would have stopped to help, I'm sure of it. He was that sort of guy.

The thing I noticed most about being back in the country again when there was *not* a war going on is that I could actually hear things without parsing them for trouble, says Cat. I mean, I could actually hear birds and insects and lizards at night without unconsciously but intently listening for metallic sounds, which meant trouble, or unusual sounds, which meant trouble. I realized, after walking for a couple of weeks, that I wasn't listening for trouble. It had taken me years to not listen for trouble without thinking about not listening, you know what I mean? But even now when a plane or a helicopter comes over I look to see where it is and where it is going and how far I am from cover. Even now. It's like a war is a language that you have to learn to speak, and then you stop speaking it, but it's there inside you forever and ever, and once in a while some of the words come up to the surface again.

In the end, wars are just not very good ideas, says Cat. I don't know anything about anything but I know that. People argue about whether we should have wars or not, but I think that's missing the point, the point isn't to not have them, you can't not have wars, people aren't like that, they will always want to fight about something, the point is to have wars that work better. You want to design a war that works out for everybody. Think of it as a heating and ventilation problem, tempers get hot and have to be cooled, how can that be done? I think chess games are the better ways to settle disputes, but no one listens to me about that. The Stork used to say that we should settle international disputes with soccer matches, but I have seen some very bloody soccer matches. No, I am pretty sure chess is the answer. But no one listens to me.

People ask me what it was like to be a soldier in a war, and I have never yet found any good answer to that question, says Cat. Wars are all the same and all different. Some things are true, though. I never met a soldier who really cared as much about beating the enemy as he did about not getting hurt and not letting his friends get hurt. That's pretty much all you care about when you're inside a war. After that we just wanted to have enough to eat and a good place to sleep and to not get wet or cold or sick. We just wanted to get through it. I never met a soldier who really and truly wanted to fight someone in the other army. You would only use your weapons because you had to, to avoid getting hurt. Anybody who really wanted to fight someone else was crazy, and we stayed away from him, because he would sure enough get in a fight. We just wanted to get out of there. We were just working, that's all. It was a job you had to do. Everyone had opinions, sure, and ideas about politics and governments, and you couldn't be in a war without disliking the other army for trying to hurt you and your friends, and the longer the war went on the more we hated them and they hated us, because people kept getting hurt. But it's not like anything you ever saw in real life, a war. You just keep going through it and hope no one you know gets hurt. It's like my father said, wars are like countries you travel through and don't know the language or the land or anything, and all you want to do is find a way out of there.

I can tell you what war smells like, though, says Cat. I sure know *that.* It smells mostly like oil. There are a lot of other smells that once you smell them in a war you never forget them, like the smell of a lot of sweating frightened men in a little space like a truck, and the smell of men's feet after they have not washed their feet for weeks and weeks, and the smell of all different sorts of mud, and the smell of things burning, and the smell of dead people and dead animals, but mostly what war smells like is oil and gas and fuel and grease. War is a sort of engineering problem and all engineering problems at some point are about oil. Trust me on this one.

One thing I should say about my travels, says Cat, is that there were a lot of sad things to see, but those are not the things that come first to mind when you ask me about my travels. Isn't that interesting? I mean, when you ask me what was it like, the first things that come to mind are that salty bread that the chicken man's granddaughter made, and the boy with a mouse on a string, and the way people sat in concentric circles around the tree where that religion was born, things like that. You wonder why some things stick in your mind and some not, and why some things have higher priority in remembering than other things. For example one of the sad things that I saw all the time in the cities and towns I walked through was mold on walls. It seemed to me no one cleaned and washed and painted the walls of old buildings, and time and time again I saw mold slowly taking down a lovely old building. That was sad. And there was a tired smell in the cities and towns, probably from the mold. And very rarely, in cities and towns, did I see a river or a stream that looked very clean. Now, out in the country, the rivers and streams generally seemed clean, but not in the cities, in the cities people were using them for sewers, and no one seemed to care or even notice. That's a sad thing. I tell my boys that clean water in the second most important thing in the whole world, after kindness.

You keep asking me about what I think about wars, says Cat, but the true answer to your question is that I have only been in a corner of one small war, so I don't know so much. Nor was I paying close attention to the nature of the thing at that time. I was busy not getting killed then. Now, since then, yes, of course, I have thought about wars a lot, and pondered and ruminated, and meditated and considered, and I have read a lot, and listened to a lot of people who have been in them or started them or tried to make them end, and I conclude that a war is a kind of animal, really. It's totally natural. For as long as there have been beings of whatever kind there have been wars between and among them. It's just the way it is. Everyone complains and moans about wars but they are part of the way things are. We conduct wars on plants and animals so as to have something to eat, and we war on the land so we make it work for us, we enslave it really, and we make water do what

59

we want with dams and canals and sprinklers and plumbing, and we make wars on other people to grab their land, and other people make war on us to grab the land from us, and that's the way it is. Any person who says why, there should be no wars! I say what would you do if a man came to rape your daughter, would you have a war with him? You bet you would. So there it is. I am not saying that we cannot someday graduate to a way to not have wars like we have them now, but I am saying that you have to use real words and be honest about wars. Every thing is in a war somehow all the time. you might as well be honest about it. Maybe being honest is the first step toward graduating to some new way.

This sounds all philosophish, says Cat, and I am no philosopher. But my father used to say that there was no evil, there was only insufficient or uncertain or immature love, and I think that is silly talk. There are a lot of evil things and evil ideas and evil acts. I have seen some. You have to be honest about that. So that is one reason we have wars, because sometimes, yes, you do have to fight against the evil things. But most wars are just confusions and greed let loose. Like the war I was in, that was really just one set of people wanting to be the boss and another set of people saying no, *we* will be the boss, and neither side having the brains to figure out a way to solve the disagreement without children being raped and women having their guts strewn across the road and men's heads floating in rivers and me losing a foot in a swamp. This is a terrible way to solve disagreements but we are not as smart as we think we are, in the long view. But also one thing that annoys me is when people use words like honor and courage and bravery and self-determination and national pride and things like that, which so often those words just mean children being murdered, when you think about it, you know what I mean?

Where was I on my trip? says Cat. O yes, in the cave. Well, I left the cave and headed south again as fast as I could go. One time I rode on a boat, one time in a wagon, one time a bus. I began to head up into the mountains, and there began to be a lot of rain. I remember passing through a village where people told me a woman lived there who had married a bear, she and the bear lived outside of town, and I remember passing through some country where there wasn't a single blade of grass, nor a single insect, or bird, or anything living whatsoever, that was an eerie place. I have no idea what happened there and I went through it as fast as I could walk. It was all completely flat, as if the ground had been carefully rolled and tended to, but everywhere you looked was the same gray color, and not a weed, not a sound, lived there. There was just the road going through it and flat gray ground with nothing as far as you could see. I remember finally I walked past that place and plants and insects and birds and sounds never sounded so good. I asked people at the next village what that place was all about but no one would answer my questions. Most remarkable.

# VII

Here and there as I walked along I could feel my foot calling to me, says Cat. Messages came to me, is the best way I can explain it. People would point in a direction suddenly when I was hesitating which way to go, or someone would say something that sounded right at the moment I needed to choose a direction, or I would have a sure feeling suddenly, when paused at a crossroads. It's hard to explain.

People say to me, all this for a foot? and it's hard for me to explain to them that all the parts of you are what make you, yes? Of course we take for granted having all our parts, when we have them, but then when we lose something, that's when we pay attention to it. you know this in your own life in so many ways, yes? When you lose a love that's when you really think about how much it meant to you. Why don't we think about that all the time that we have the love? I don't know. I think about this a lot with my wife and sons. I try to look at them every day and see them as I would see them if they weren't there anymore, you know? That's how it was with my foot. I never thought about it when I had it, it was just the part of me that helped me walk and swim and run and kick my brothers and soccer balls, but then as soon as it was gone I thought about it all the time. You wouldn't believe how much I thought about my foot after it left. Sure I thought about why it left, and whose fault it was, and how I could get revenge, and why the other guys in my patrol didn't stop for me, and things like that, but after a while what I thought most was what a good foot it had been, and I hard hardly even noticed, what a shame.

People say, o, maybe losing your foot was actually a gift, it taught you patience and endurance and to see more clearly and savor the things of life, but that is silly talk, who would rather not have a foot than have one? Not me. Which is why I went to find it, you know.

When my sons were born, says Cat, do you know what I did more than anything else?

I just lay there looking at them, all the parts that worked, their eyes and toes and fingers and feet and tongues, all so amazing. Our one son was born and I could have stared at him all day if I didn't have to go to work. Then our other son was born, just as amazing as the first son. You could never believe a whole new person would come out of your wife if you didn't see it with your own eyes. And everyone is always talking about how tiny and helpless babies are, but you know what I think is the most amazing part? Their amazing parts. I mean, most of the time most parts work in most babies. Isn't that the most remarkable thing? I cannot think of anything more remarkable than that, really, in the whole world. *New people are made every minute! Ha!*

I kept thinking that I saw the chief of the soldiers again, here and there, says Cat. One time I thought I saw him in the door of a church, staring at me, and one time a man passing by me on a bicycle sure looked like him, and another time I woke up in a field and there was a man looking at me who I was so convinced it was him that I snatched my stick and jumped up ready to fight. But none of them were him.

That religion that I saw being born one day, says Cat, you wouldn't believe how fast it spread through the countryside. One day it was a huddle of people sitting by a tree and telling stories about the young woman, and the next there were little shrines and ceremonies everywhere you went. It was a most remarkable thing. Even in the time I was there in the country you could see the religion changing a little from what it had been in the beginning. It started out being about the young woman and the tree that grew where she had vanished, and then it became about this certain kind of tree, people began to pay a lot of money to get that kind of tree, and people started businesses to bring that kind of tree into the country, and build little shrines and shelters around the tree, and start little food shacks to feed the people who were coming to sit by the tree, and then one man in one place planted a tree and put a wall around it and charged money for people to come through the gate and touch the tree. That was interesting. And where people used to tell a lot of stories about the young woman who had vanished, no one told stories about her anymore, now there were a lot of stories about who had been healed by

66

touching the tree, and how if you touched that sort of tree you could have babies if you were barren, and things like that.

Speaking of trees, says Cat, one day when I was in the mountains I came to a place where people had been nailed to trees during the war. Men women and children. You can't believe someone would ever nail a child's hands to a tree but – believe it. I saw it with my eyes, the trees, the nails, the skeleton hands. You can't believe anyone would ever do that to anyone else, but it happened. There was a man there who told me what happened. I don't know the rest of the story there, why that happened or how much, just what he told me. That's enough to know. That was one of those days when I stayed where I was for a long time. I couldn't go on for a while. I am not much of a praying guy but that day I prayed, o yes. Praying doesn't do anything you can see, you know, but sometimes that's all you can do. I think praying is mostly for the people who do the praying, it makes them feel better, you know, but sometimes there is nothing to say except to say a prayer. Doesn't matter what kind of prayer. Any prayer will do, on a day like that day.

People ask me, did I kill anybody in the war, says Cat, did I do unbelievably cruel things, and I say yes, I did. I shot seven men that I remember, and threw bombs and things that certainly killed more men. I shot one man who was crawling away from where we were fighting, that was probably the most cruel thing I did. There's not much for me to say about that. I was in one army and he was in another and he was wounded and I wasn't, and he tried to get away and I didn't let him. That's what happened. There's not much more to say. Everything that you could say now, it wouldn't matter.

Sometimes I think people actually like to lose their tempers and have arguments about politics because they are afraid they would like to kill people if they were stuck in a war like soldiers are, says Cat. That's what I think. I think a lot of people are afraid they would like to kill, rather than not. One thing I learned as a soldier was that the people who are most afraid are the loudest. Any fellow you met in the war who was talking about bravery and courage and attacking the enemy and defending the motherland and right and wrong and moral purpose and things like that, you tried to stay away from him. We were all mostly just trying to get through the war. I try to explain this to people but either I am not very good at explaining or they are very good at listening. Wars are just wars. People have wars because they are people. Some people say well, let's just *stop* having the wars, let us be non-violent, and that sounds like a good idea, but human beings have to have some kinds of war. This is why I advocate chess games instead of wars, but no one listens to me.

That's another thing I should say, says Cat, I played a lot of chess when I was walking. Pretty much every village and town has a place where people play chess, either in shops or in parks or sometimes in schools, and one great thing about chess is that it's a language, you know? So you can speak to people without saying any words. I can't tell you how often that happened, that I walked into a park and got into a game and matched wits with someone and then the person smiled and shook hands and asked me where I was from and where I was going and did I need something to eat, things like that. Chess is a wonderful thing. If I was in charge of schools I would teach it like math or science of storytelling. Maybe if everyone played chess we could have different kinds of wars. That's what I think, anyway.

But some things are beyond wars, says Cat. For example I'll tell you a story I never told anyone before. I bet only ten men in the world know this story and probably a few of those men are gone now. There was a man in my patrol who couldn't resist raping people. Every time he had the chance he would commit that crime. Well, in a war you have a lot of chances to do things that few people know about, because you are always moving around and hiding and getting lost and getting into fights where no one knows if anyone else got hurt or not for a while, and in wars there are always people around who are helpless and don't have any weapons, so sometimes things happen. Well, this man in our patrol, we saw what he was like pretty quickly, and for one reason or another pretty much every other man in the patrol told him to stop, some men because they were appalled and some men because they thought he was adding danger to our situation, but he wouldn't stop, so finally we got him one day and shot the end off his peter. That's just what happened. So that's what I mean when I say some things are beyond wars. If you added up all the bullets we shot among those ten guys who were in the patrol, over all the years we were in the war, they would almost all be bullets we shot against the other army, or shot to get food so we could stay healthy to fight the other army, except that one bullet. That bullet was about something beyond the war. So.

I never did see the chief of soldiers again, says Cat, but one day yes, I did see the older of the two soldiers who had brought me to the headquarters. Not the young one who let me go but the other one. He was in a truck of soldiers going past me on the road and I looked up just as he looked down and we caught each other's eye. One thing I learned over the years was to never look up like that as soldiers or policemen were going by, if you don't see them they don't see you, but something, I don't know, a sound, something, made me look up, and he saw me, and my soul was cold. He didn't say anything, or stare, or shout, and I wasn't sure if he remembered, but as soon as I could I set off straight west instead of south, and put as many miles between me and that road as I could. I spent one day in a library, reading and writing letters, and one day at a school, where I worked a day clearing brush in exchange for food, and another day at a convent, where believe it or not they gave me peanut-butter-and-jelly sandwiches, one of the nuns there just loved them, she was so happy to see my face when she handed me one! Ha! Then I turned and went on south again, up into the mountains.

# VIII

I went up and up and up, says Cat. Those mountains don't look very high, there's no snow on them or anything, but they are steep and dark and folded and there are a lot of secret ravines and remote corners. The people who live up there have been there for about a million years by themselves and they have different languages and customs. I think the people up there are like the mountains, they are secret and remote. Sometimes I wonder if where people live shapes how people are, you know?

Anyway I walked and got rides where I could and I came finally to a town that sounded familiar but I couldn't remember how or why I knew the name. I stopped there for tea to listen to my memory for a while, you know how sometimes you know something but you have to wait for it to hatch into words? Plus I had lost the direction of my foot and needed to just sit quietly and listen to the air for a while. So I did that.

Finally I remembered how I knew the name of that town. My mother's father had been sent there after the war, he and the people in his village were sent to this town to populate it again, because everyone who was there in the war was killed, no one was left, and the government didn't want the town to be famous for being empty, so my grandfather and his neighbors had to pack up and move there, even though they were from down in the valley and didn't know how to live up in the mountains where it was foggy and cold. My grandfather was very old when this happened and we were not allowed to see him or write to him or anything, so I had not seen him since before the war, when I was a boy. But maybe he was here still, so I went looking.

I went to the school and the library, those are always the best places to ask after people in a town, and then to the shops where food was being sold, those are usually friendly places with news, but I avoided the police station.

Finally I found the firemen's house, and a fireman there said he thought my grandfather was still alive, he was in a house for poor old people in the blue part of the town. That town was divided up into colored parts for some reason, red and yellow and orange and green and purple and blue, and all the old men and women who had no money and no relatives lived in a falling-down-house in the blue section of town, so I went there.

And there was my grandfather! He knew me right away and didn't even look surprised! Ah, Cat, he said, what a pleasure to see your face again, are you missing a foot? He was incredibly old and thin and tiny, he said he was getting smaller every day and soon would be gone altogether, and he said he was more than a hundred years old, but he was quick-minded and funny and his voice was like water to a thirsty man. I sat on the edge of his bed and we talked and talked. What a wonderful man he was! He had been the best grandfather to me when I was a small boy, both of my grandfathers were just the most excellent grandfathers, but one died and the other was sent away into the mountains, but here we were! What a great day that was with my grandfather!

We won't have very much time together, said my grandfather, so let me say some important things. First of all I love you and I always will no matter where I go. Your grandmother, you know, she is behind you all the time. She is behind your right ear and I will be behind your left ear. If you need us just call for us and we will be there. I know you have two sons and a wonderful wife. Your grandmother talks to me still, you know.

I should say, says Cat, that my mother's mother, my grandfather's wife, had died many years before this, when I was just little, barely walking, and all I remember of her was sitting in her lap, and that she wore red dresses all the time, and smelled like coconut.

Another thing, said my grandfather, is that I want you to remember everything you can. Remembering is very powerful. It's the way things and people stay alive. No matter where you go, try to remember this country and the way it was, so that no one can ever kill it completely. Will you do that for me? I will help you. Remember the one hundred kinds of soup we have, and elephants who smile when you scratch them with a stick, and the tiny altars in little rooms in the backs of our houses. Remember the way we rode bicycles through the fringe of the ocean sometimes, the back tire kicking up a pheasant's tail of salt water, and everyone laughing and getting wet! Remember when the rains finally came and it felt like the sea was falling out of the sky and everyone went out in the street and turned their faces up to the water and said thank you god! Remember the way some people built boats that were houses and they lived on the rivers and every once in a while they would sail away in their house! Remember the snakes so big they sometimes would catch and eat a horse, and how good it is to eat a fresh mango with a fresh fish, and the way the cranes jump and leap when they are courting each other, and the famous sisters who were the queens of our country a million years ago, and the way old people like me learned to write with slivers of wood on leaves of trees, and the old man in our village who all his clothes were made from enormous leaves, and the way thousands of people lived in tunnels under the country during the wars, and the way owls teased each other at night, and about the brilliant monkey who was elected mayor in a village in the south, and how gifts for new brides are always wrapped in red, and how there is a religion in the south that says all comedians are saints, and how the best governments have lots of poets, and how puppeteers made their puppets dance in the middle of the river with long sticks, and how the stones in our fireplace were either male or female, and how if a man wears a peach blossom on his shirt you know you can trust him, and how all our rivers have different colors, and how otters will talk to you if you are patient and gentle with them and give them fish to eat, and how one time a government burned all the musical instruments in the country but new ones were born in the bellies of trees and given to us by the trees one summer night, and how some men wear hawks as hats, and how when people vote they say yes with their left hand and no with their right, and how you can use six different musical tones when you speak our language, and how every lake is ruled by an old turtle, and how when a baby turns two years old she is surrounded by tools and implements and she chooses the shape of her life, and how we think chess is the greatest game in the history of the world, and how sometimes people who shout too much have to go to jail for a day,

78

and how there are worms and tigers who are saints as well as people who are saints.

Yes, grandfather.

And how married women wear strong colors, and blue is the color of tolerance, and yellow is the color of virtue, and how a woman in the north once had a hundred children, and how once we had a king whom no one ever saw for the whole span of his life, and how one time a man in the south built a whole house out of tree sap, and how if you watch carefully at night you can see octopuses dance on the floor of the sea, and how there is an island where people eat the nests of birds, and how the bees are your friends if you are polite to them, and how your grandmother had a magic hat that if you wore it you could understand any language, and how people in the mountains smoke pipes bigger than they are, and how in the old days whenever you had a new baby you would add a room to the house so some houses after a hundred years had fifty rooms or more, and how when young people marry they eat honey and salt to remind themselves that love is both sweet and sweaty, and how when someone dies you leave a knife on his belly so he can fend off the spirits, and how there was a priest once who ate only coconuts his whole life, and how many animals are our uncles to this day, and how one time many years ago there was a woman priest who could make people out of clay, but one summer it got so hot that all her clay people melted.

Yes, grandfather.

And how sometimes people when they are really thirsty take a fruit and punch a hole in it and insert a straw and drink right from the belly of the beast so to speak, said my grandfather, and how my own father's father made the greatest fish sauce in the history of the world about twice a year, everything went right and all the ingredients were perfect and the table would glow, you remember? and how sometimes in the places where someone was blown up by a mine left over from the war people put a leg bone on a stick to mark that spot, and how there are places deep in the country where churches and temples have been so overgrown with the roots of great trees that you can't walk into them anymore and only the tree knows what it's like inside that church, and how so many statues have such gentle smiles that after a while you wonder what they are smiling about, and how sometimes in the war if an army was going to kill a lot of people all at once in the same place they would put loudspeakers in the trees and play music really loud so no one would hear people screaming, and how your grandmother saved that baby eagle that time by keeping it in a pot by the stove so it would be warm in the cold time, you remember that, remember how enormous that bird grew?

I do, grandfather.

So what happened to your foot? he asked.

I explained that I had lost it in the swamp during the war, and was now engaged in finding it again, and he smiled and said it would most probably have gone down toward the sea. We spent another hour together telling stories and laughing and drinking tea and eating the little berries grandfather had loved since he was a small boy, and then he said he had to sleep, being more than a hundred years old, and we kissed each other seven times and I went on. That was such a great day! He was the best grandfather anyone could ever have!

# IX

You keep asking me about being in the war, says Cat, so I will tell you some cold hard facts, and we will see if that helps explain anything whatsoever at all.

I was in the army for eleven months, one week, and two days, two and a half days really, until I stepped on the mine and lost my foot and had to hop out of there. Most of the time I was in the army we operated in a large valley relatively near the sea. I never saw the ocean while I was in the army but gulls and seabirds would fly over the valley a good deal so I knew salt water was nearby. Learned that from my grandfather, who taught me to pay attention to who lived where, for example low wet places have different insects and birds than high dry places, and et cetera.

The valley where we were was not country that I had known previously, so I was perhaps a little more attentive to it, you know how when you are in a strange place your ears and eyes and smell sharpens, it must be a function of curiosity or maybe fear. Certainly it was partly fear in my case, because the other army was there trying to kill us, and every sound was a letter in a new alphabet, you know what I mean? The situation in the valley was that the other army had two major supply roads along the walls of the valley, one on either side, supplying the other parts of their army, and my army's job there in the valley was to obstruct those roads insofar as possible. Of course every time we broke a road they fixed it, and they were always attacking us to keep us away from the roads, so we all spent a lot of time hiding from each other. Mostly I suppose both armies were mostly lost all the time. The valley was mostly a dense forest with swamps at the bottom. In the swamps there were leopards and panthers and snakes big enough to eat horses. Also twice we saw a tiny rhinoceros, pretty much the last thing you expected to see while wending your way through a swamp in the morning in a war. We

84

spent a lot of time wandering around. There were ten of us in our patrol, and our army had ten patrols our size in the valley at any one time, and we spent pretty much all our time slipping back and forth across the valley and trying to obstruct the enemy's supply roads. We blew them up with explosives, we set traps, we diverted streams to wash them out, we blocked them by felling trees, we tried everything we could. We learned a lot about engineering by trying to unengineer roads, you know what I mean? And of course all the time the enemy was trying to catch us, and prevent us from messing with their roads, so they would lay in wait for us, and we would lay in wait for them, and if you made a mistake you got shot, that's pretty much the way it was.

You know the first thing I remember when I think about laying traps for the other army on their roads? The time we dug a pit and put stakes in it and one of their soldiers fell into the pit and was impaled. It was like a war from a thousand years ago.

Two of the men in my patrol had been trained in military tactics and ordnance but the rest of us were mostly just boys, that is the story of pretty much ever war, a couple of men have an idea of how to go about things and the rest are just boys with major weapons. All wars are fought by boys sent by old men, that is the way it is. Now, people will say, that other army was invading us, and this is true, no one invited them into the valley or into the country, and that is one reason we fought them, but another reason is that we had to, that was the law, that you had to be in the army, and sometimes I think that maybe wars start backwards, you know, that if you make an army, then you have to have a war for the army to fight. But I am also not totally stupid, and the fact is that this other army wanted to make a new government, and my family and friends and neighbors didn't particularly want a new government, so there was a war.

My patrol got pretty good at tactics, all things considered. We learned how to approach objectives silently and with crossed lines of fire. We learned how to conduct operations in the dark. We learned how to move efficiently in the rain. We mostly moved at night and slept during the day. We learned to do without a lot of equipment that we thought we needed at the beginning of the war. We learned to eat mostly what we could find in the forest. We learned to sleep whenever we had a moment. We learned how to steal whatever we needed. We learned how to fix whatever needed to be fixed whether or not we had the right tools or parts. We learned that the feet are perhaps the most important parts of a soldier's body. You wouldn't believe how important it is to keep your feet healthy in a war. If your feet hurt or are sick you just are no good whatsoever. One thing I learned in the war was total respect for feet. We take them so for granted, yes? And I don't say this as a man who lost one. I say this with real admiration for the engineering and design. All your weight depends on these two intricate structures, composed on many small bones and moving parts. Isn't that remarkable? Do you ever really stop and consider the amazing things that your feet are? I don't think that we do. You can bounce on them, jump from them, balance on them, spin on them, point them, rotate them, pick things up with them, swim with them, kick things, balance balls and children, hang by them, paint them, and wear untold numbers of shoes and slippers on them. They carry all sorts of weight. Sometimes they are the first parts of people to emerge into the world. Sometimes they are the last parts of people to be cremated. It's almost like they are alive by themselves down there, wiggling around, talking to each other in sign language or something. They are most remarkable creatures, when you think about it, and I have certainly had occasion to think about it, yes?

There were a lot of times in the war that I didn't think I was going to stay alive, says Cat, and there were even a few times that I didn't see much reason to keep living anyway. I never told anyone about that but I might as well be honest about it now. For the former there were a few times when I was in real danger of being killed, and for the latter there were some moments when I sat there thinking what was the point, I would probably be killed anyway, and I had no wife or children or money, so I might as well just get it over with, or conclude to escape, maybe slip out of the valley at night and down to the ocean and steal a boat and vanish, you know? But that was silly talk All the reasons I could say that I never did any of those things would be lies, because the reason I didn't do that was my friends in the patrol. I couldn't leave them down one man. That would be cheating them. You can't cheat your friends. Plus I was very young in the war, all of twenty years old, and when you are twenty you can't stay sad, there's too much interesting things. At least there was for me. No one says that about wars, that they are *interesting*, but it's so. No one wants to admit that. All the things that people say about wars are true, they are stupid and cruel and exhausting and terrifying and despairing and horrendous and twisted and squirming and foolish, but they're also *fascinating*. Maybe that's why they have been around so long, yes?

Well, says Cat, I actually have to go to the foot store today to get a backup foot, I broke my wooden foot recently and have been wearing the rubber one again, I was coming down a ladder the other day and must have stepped wrong and broke the foot but I didn't know it until I came home and took my boot off and my foot fell out, ha!

Anyway a story I wanted to tell was about my other grandfather, my father's father. We did not know him very well because he was married to several women and had relationships with several others, and things were awkward with him. My father called him a butterfly because he wore flitted from flower to flower and like to wear bright clothes. He liked to get married, my grandfather, because he liked to be in love, but as soon as love went from honey to salt he would quit and find somebody else to fall in love with, and so on. He wanted to be happy all the time, my grandfather, and you can't fault a man for that, I guess. But things were awkward with him in my family, and no one felt like they could lean on him at all, because he might just quit and go looking somewhere else for whatever it was he was looking for.

I guess talking about my other grandfather reminded me of this grandfather. I don't even know what happened to this grandfather. He left one day and never came back and no one ever talked about him again. I don't even have any more stories about him. Isn't that a sad thing, to not have any stories to tell about somebody?

But I will tell you one last story today, says Cat, and it is the answer to the question you have asked me every day for weeks, about heroism. I have thought long and hard about that. There were some men I knew who were unbelievably brave, and whenever I think about bravery, or hear the word thrown around casually on television or the radio or the newspapers I think about those men, but heroism is different, I think. You can be brave when you are called to be, when the chance presents itself, but a hero is brave all the time, in ways he or she probably doesn't know. Maybe not knowing is one of the definitions of heroism, yes? Anyway the most heroic person I ever met in the war was a woman who sold her body twice a day every day for years and years, how do you like that? That surprises you, yes? But she had no husband, he was dead, and her father and mother were dead, and her brothers and sisters were dead, and everyone she knew was dead or gone, and her village was destroyed, and the land where she lived was destroyed, and she had no money to travel anywhere else—but she had two little children, and she cared for those children with all her might and with every drop of energy she had. She got them food and shelter and safety day after day, in circumstances that were worse than any hell you could imagine, so I think she is a hero. Some people would say she was a whore or a criminal or a loose woman or a sinner. I don't know about that. All I know is that she had two children and she found them food and a little shed to live in and she kept them out of the way of the war. So I think she is a hero. But what do I know?

One day, says Cat, I met a boy who was simple, and we traveled together for several days. He had no name, this boy, and all he had in the way of possessions was a stick like mine, and a spoon and a bowl, and a large cloth that he used for all sorts of things, a tent in the rain, a blanket in the night, a coat in the cold, a tarpaulin with which to catch water when he was thirsty. He was a most remarkable boy. He had no words that I remember but he laughed a great deal. Also he was missing a foot and when I asked him what had happened to it he just shrugged. He was about my size, and after we traveled together for a few days I concluded to give him the rubber foot the woodworker had made for me. I had worn it for quite a while now and had enjoyed having it, and there he was without a foot, so I just gave it to him. I was used to not having a foot, after all, more than he was, and you should have seen his face when I attached the foot for him! What a face! You never saw such a happy boy! I thought he was going to float into the heavens because he was so happy! He danced around and around and got so dizzy he had to lie down for a while. I had to laugh.

After that I kept my eyes peeled for some more rubber to try to make another foot, because I had paid attention when the wood-worker made mine, and I have a little skill with engineering and carpentry, and after a while I found the right kind of tire and I made a decent foot from the rubber. Not as good as the one the woodworker made, but not too bad. Good enough for the moment. I put the thought in the back of my mind that perhaps circling back around to the woodworker's house would be a good idea eventually, because he was a very good craftsman, that fellow. Boy, could he make good feet.

We traveled along better after that, the boy and I, says Cat. By now we were deep in the mountains and the trails were thin and high. One time we fell in with a group of monks who were traveling also. They walked in single file even when the trail was wide, and one of them told me they had done this since time immemorial, because back in the old time when they walked two by two as God instructed, some monks were walking along a trail very high in the mountains and one monk got so furiously angry at another as they were walking that he shoved the second fellow off the trail, but lost his balance and fell himself, so that they both fell thousands of feet to their deaths. I said that lesson of that story was not to lose your temper, yes? But he said no, the lesson of the story was the walk in single file, which they did ever after.

Another time when I was traveling with that boy, says Cat, we came to a town where everyone was gathered at the playing field, an enormous crowd, it must have been every man woman and child for miles around, all together at the sporting place, and silent as a church. We stood with the crowd, curious. I think there were thousands of people there, no one of them making a sound. They were waiting for something that was hugely important for them but we didn't have the slightest idea what it was. A most remarkable moment. Then in the corner of the crowd a man stepped gently onto the field and the crowd burst into a unbelievable roar. I don't know if he was a player or an elder or what, but everyone was so happy to see him that we were happy too, you know that feeling when everyone else's feeling seeps into you? A wonderful feeling. Dangerous too. I remember that he had a green shirt and that he seemed shy, that fellow.

We had some other adventures, that boy and I, says Cat. One time we helped build a fish weir, do you know what that is, a sort of a trap for fish, this was in a very cold fast little river in the mountains, and the people who were building it talked with their hands, they had a whole language with their hands and fingers, a most remarkable thing, and this was one of those times when I saw that the boy wasn't simple at all, he learned their finger language quick as a blink and he was even making jokes with his fingers, he would make a gesture lightning-quick and they would all laugh. I felt like I was the simple one there, you know?

Another time we helped a school with their heating, ventilation, and air-conditioning needs, this was totally by accident, we were just sitting under a tree one day resting when we got to talking to a teacher who told me that the boiler in that school had been dead for years, so the school was freezing in the winter and boiling in the summer, so I looked at the boiler and all that was the problem was valves and ducts. This was a fairly small problem and I did what I could and the boiler came to life like magic. You should have seen those kids when heat came through the ducts in their classroom! It still makes me laugh to think about them bouncing around the classroom. I bet it took that teacher three days to calm them down enough for lessons. One girl said to me that now her great dream was to be a heating, ventilation, and air-conditioning person like me. This makes me laugh. I told my sons about that girl one time and one of my sons said I should start a missionary society of heating, ventilation, and air-conditioning people, and send missions all over the world, and elevate the level of heating, ventilation, and air-conditioning everywhere. You could do worse things, yes? We would have blue robes, perhaps, with a shoulder patch in the shape of a screwdriver, yes?

Another time the boy got sick, this was

when we were in a place where it was cold and foggy all the time, the people said, and he couldn't even walk, so he lay down right in the road, but a woman came along who said he could rest at her house. He rested there for two days and got his legs back under him. I wrote letters while he slept, and the woman said she would find a way to start them on their way to my wife and sons. It might take a while, she said, but she would find a way. The letters might get home after you do, she said, wouldn't that be funny, it would be like your voice from another time and place being caught in these little paper packages, and maybe you all open the letters together at the kitchen table at home, and your voice comes out so surprised to see you! The last person your voice expected to see was *you*!

Another time, says Cat, we were stopped by policemen, and brought to their headquarters, and things didn't look good, I was fearful especially because of my dealings with the chief of the soldiers back down the road, but the chief of these policemen knew the finger language of the people we had helped with the fish trap, and he and the boy had a long talk with their hands and pretty soon they let us go. I remember the way they bowed to us as we left, very courteous fellows.

We went on, says Cat, the boy and I, and finally we came to a parting of the ways. He wanted to stay in the mountains, he liked it there, and I needed to keep going, so we shook hands and parted. He wanted to give me his cloak but there are some gifts you cannot accept, yes? But you must accept some sort of a gift from a person who wishes to give you a gift, so eventually the boy taught me a little of the finger language, to have in case I needed it in the future, he taught me to say *good morning*, and *have mercy*, and *how can I help you*, and *may I have a glass of water*, those are the basics in any language, of course. I still have those words in my hand and now my sons have them too. It's interesting, isn't it, how languages travel from place to place like people do. You wonder which came first, people or their languages. Maybe the languages wandered around looking for people to speak them, you know? Or maybe languages invented people so as to have someone to be spoken by. Maybe God is a language looking for people to speak him, yes?

I think about that boy once in a while, says Cat, and I hope he is well. He was a very intelligent boy and I hope he is still in the mountains. I think that was the place where he was supposed to be. The place you are supposed to be isn't necessarily where you are from, but then again there are a lot of people who are always looking for the right place and never finding it, just as there are a lot of people who keep looking for the right person to be with and never finding that person. You wonder sometimes if some people are the tribe of always-looking people. But not that boy. I think he found the place where he was supposed to be. A most remarkable boy.

# XI

I went on, says Cat, and now again I was by myself, traveling for some days, slowly coming down out of the mountains. I am not sure quite how long that was. By now I had learned who and where to ask about my foot when I came to a town. Churches and chapels and temples and stupas and monasteries and abbeys and convents were good places, men and women there were interested in what I was doing and not so skeptical or dismissive, and schools were also good places, teachers and children were interested and often very firm about what direction I should go, and generally policemen were good to talk to. Soldiers were not so good to talk to, they had business to attend to, and shops selling things other than food were not the best places to go, for some reason. But shops selling food, they were good. Something about food makes people interested in talking to strangers, I guess.

Sometimes I took buses, and once a train from one city to another when I found a ticket sitting on the head of a statue in a park, and several times in carts and wagons, and once a mule, but I got off that mule pretty quickly for reasons you will understand if you have ever ridden a horse or a mule and you are not used to it, you know what I mean? Ah, I see you do. How many times have you ridden a horse? Just the once? For the same reason as I got off the mule? Yes? I don't see how people can ride mules and horses and burros, personally. Did you know there are people who ride pigs and cows and oxen? Are there people who ride deer and elk and bears and giraffes? People must have tried to do that. People must have tried to ride every animal there is, I suppose, whales and tigers and eagles. Not me! No eagles for me!

Now you got me all laughing, says Cat, and I will lose my story if you don't stop laughing. Anyway I was coming down from the mountains, traveling alone, and now I was really missing my wife and sons, and thinking

102

that my trip was silly and crazy and stupid, what actually would I *do* with my foot if I ever found it, and what kind of idiot goes looking for his foot anyway long after the war, and what chance did I have of finding it anyway, surely it had splintered into a million pieces there in the swamp like everyone said, and all that anyone would ever find of it would be a tiny shard the size of a tooth, a child would dig it up fifty years from now while playing in the back yard, and he would show it to his father, who would pronounce it absolutely a horse's tooth, and the child would say wow, and keep it in a box until he forgot about it, and then someone, probably the mother, would throw it away out in the yard again, where it would wait patiently for another child to find it in fifty years, and so on.

That was the kind of thing I was thinking as I came down from the mountains, says Cat, but then one day I met a very interesting woman and we had a most interesting discussion and things turned in most interesting ways.

I don't know how old she was. She was younger than me but not by too much. She had dark hair and dark eyes and was lovely, but none of those things were the things you noticed first about her, first you noticed that she was sort of electrically charged and then you noticed that she was happy in herself, you know what I mean? We talked for a long time. This was at a tea shop. She was easy to talk to. I think this is because she smiled and laughed, yes? So words and ideas went more easily between us. We got to talking, and I explained why I was there, and what I was doing, and she didn't laugh or say that I was crazy, so I liked that, and then she told me about her husband and their children, who were still little. One of her children had visions and shivers and shakes and they were not sure if the girl was sick or holy.

Sometimes that's the same thing, I said. Or maybe holy people have thinner skins or something.

That could be, she said, and we got to talking about how holy people were either children or a lot like children, and the more unlike children they got, the less holy they got, until finally someone who used to be holy was only working in business like everyone else.

I really liked her and she really liked me, and when I say that I don't mean in the lover way, although who knows what would have happened if we had met each other in different years and different ways? But that kind of question is silly talk. Everyone could meet everyone else in an infinite number of ways. But as my friend the Stork used to say maybe dreaming about other lovers is the way that you have other lovers without having them in the real world, yes? But then he was one of those guys who was always looking at girls and thinking how they would fit with him and vice versa. It was a sort of a game or meditation for him.

No, I wasn't thinking of that woman in the lover way. I think of my wife in the lover way, and have never been able to think of any other women that same way since I met my wife. My wife is just a different sort of woman and I like the sort of woman she is, which no one else is, or no one else I have met yet, anyway.

No, I was just happy to have met the woman in the tea shop, to have talked to her, to have connected to her music a little, you know? She was a good person to have entered your life, whether or not she *stayed* in your life. I felt better myself, a little deeper, like I was a lake and she was good rain and now I was a little bigger lake. She wasn't a lover, she wasn't a friend, she was just herself, I don't have any good words for how we liked each other. We just felt comfortable talking, like we had known each other a long time and didn't have masks and pasts. Boy, sometimes the right words have not been invented yet for a lot of things! Ha!

Anyway we talked happily for a while and then I said I had to keep going and she said very gently but firmly that I should walk southwest, which I did. She gave me a bottle of tea and four little cakes to take with me, and we shook hands at the door, and she said *I will ask my daughter to pray for you*, which I thought was a very kind thing to say, and I went on.

# XII

Today I am going to ask *you* questions, says Cat, because I never ask you anything about you, and you are always asking me things about me, and this doesn't seem fair. I mean, we have known each other for many years now, and many times have had tea, and many times stopped as we crossed paths and had conversations about this and that, and now we have spent all these weeks talking about the time I went to find my foot, but all these weeks when I ask you anything you just sit there smiling, with your notebook and pencil, and you never say anything, so now my turn.

How did you meet your wife? Did you want to marry anyone before her? Have you wanted to marry anyone else since you have been married to her? What does her laugh sound like? What does she smell like? Is she a good cook? When she loses her temper does she throw things? When she laughs does she throw her head back? How many children do you have? Are they polite and courteous children? Did they used to be? Do you have birds in the house? What kinds of music do you like? Have you ever been on top of a mountain? Can you swim? Are there kings and queens in your family line? Have you always worn spectacles? Did you used to be strong? What sport did you like the best? Do you like beer? How many times a day do you pray? When you see a river or a lake or a pond or the ocean do you always touch it? What is the animal of your clan or tribe of family? Did your family used to be from another country? When you write a book how do you know where to start and where to end? Is your father a storycatcher also? Have all the men in your family been storycatchers? Has your nose been broken several times, is that why it is bent sideways like that? When you were sick as a child and your mother held you what did she sing? Can you make a table with your hands? Have you ever struck a child? Have you ever fired a gun? Do you blow on your tea

108

to cool it or do you wait patiently one minute for God to cool it in the proper fashion? Do you sit in the front or the back of church? Do you know any rich people? When you commit a sin do you rub ashes on your hands? Do you use the same towel every day for your bath or do you require a fresh towel every day? When someone tells you a story how do you know if it's a true story? Are you too fascinated by lizards and geckos? Can a story that you make up out of nothing be a true story? Can a story that's made up all of facts be a false story? Did you have to go to story school to be a storycatcher? Do you ever get tired of stories? What do you do if you catch too many stories, do you throw some back? Did you ever steal a story from someone? When you are sad do you go into the forest? When someone you love dies do you sing death songs? After you cook eggs for your children do you soak the pan in hot water right away or do you let it cool down first? When you are sad do you get all your hair cut off? Have any of your children died? Have you ever been in a boat? Are you going to answer any of my questions or just sit there smiling with your notebook and pencil and say nothing?

Did you ever consider, says Cat, that you taking my story, and making it into a book for other people to read, is sort of a robbery? I mean, not from me. I am giving you the story freely, yes, and I am honored that you have asked for it, and are accepting it with such courtesy, but of course I can only give you a little of it, some corners and shreds and pieces, not all of it, so the people who read your book, they will not have the *whole* story of when I went to find my foot, so isn't that robbing them of their money? I mean, I am doing my best to remember, and you are doing your best to write it all down, but surely I am forgetting some things, and then there are a lot of things I cannot put into words in the right way, and chances are you are getting some things wrong, so really all we are doing is getting bits and parts.

For example one time I saw a heron, it was standing in a river, and from whatever angle you looked at that heron, it was a different color, you know what I mean? I walked around and around that heron and it went from green to blue to gray to cream to brown to black and then back around to green and blue again, depending on where I was standing. All the time I moved around it, astonished, it just stood there on one leg in the river. That was a most remarkable heron. And see, I just remembered that bird, I had forgotten to tell you about that bird, and there must be a thousand things like that bird, you know what I mean? Herons of every conceivable shape and size and story, you know what I mean? It's funny how many stories we don't tell when we tell a story. Maybe every story has like a thousand stories under it holding it up to the light like an iceberg or one of those long seaweeds in the ocean where a little bit is near the surface eating sunlight and all the rest of it goes down down down into the dark sea.

You know what I have been thinking? says Cat. I think we have not fully discussed and explored the idea of how the world is essentially a very large heating, cooling, and ventilation problem. Consider the many aspects of this idea. There is the physical world, which obviously is a heating, cooling, and ventilation system, and very well designed and maintained, too, with occasional serious system breakdowns. There is the emotional world, which clearly is a heating, cooling, and ventilation system also, consider how we lose our tempers, calm down, have to step out for a breath of air, need a night out with friends, drink beer, go on vacations, and things like that. There is the political world, which very consciously applies heat, distracts attention, creates smokescreens, and has outlets for people to blow off steam without really changing the system. There is the family, which waxes and wanes as far as use of energy, time together, and things like that. Isn't this interesting? You are smiling and not saying anything again. Is that because you don't understand heating, cooling, and ventilation? I can understand your reluctance to speak. It took me a long time to get the principles down but now I think I am conversant, as my sons say. Isn't that a lovely word, conversant?

You know what else I have been thinking? says Cat. I have been thinking that when I get to the end of the story about my trip, we will be at the end of our conversation, and that will be a sad day. So I have been thinking I should not tell you any more about what happened to me, because every thing I tell you is one step closer to the end. You know what I mean? Isn't it funny that we want to know the end of a story, but then we are sad when we get to the end? Why is that? So today I have decided just to try to remember little tiny things from all over my trip, not in order, and not very dramatic, just little things, and you can salt them into the story wherever you want, and we will consider that they are not advancing the story, exactly, but are little tiny parts of the story that I missed along the way. Which of course is what happens all the time with all stories, yes? So then. One day I met a man who had also been a soldier in the war and had also lost a foot but he lost his *other* foot, so we laughed to think that together we had a good pair of original feet. Another day I had the best bowl of soup I ever had ever, and then discovered it was made from lizards, ha! Another day a girl showed me some berries I had never ever seen before, even though I was born and raised in that very part of the country. Another day I watched a soccer game and found myself at the fence crying for reasons I don't know. Another day I got so unbelievably drunk that I slept out in a field and woke up in the morning all covered with dew and there was an enormous cow looking at me. That cow was tremendous. I don't think I have ever seen a cow that big before or since. I thought it was the mother of all cows, a Hindu god or something, maybe I was dead and had accidentally ended up in the wrong heaven, but then it sneezed right in my face, and I knew I was in our world! Ha!

Well, says Cat, I will tell you one more story today, and then let us take the rest of the day off, so that story will stay in your mind and mine, because it is a very excellent story. It is this: one day I helped a baby be born. I was coming down out of the mountains, down toward the sea, and I was on the road walking with my stick, when I heard a woman wailing, and went to investigate. It was a young woman in a little cabin or cottage, she was all by herself, no one around, no husband or mother or sister or anything, and she was having a baby. She was awfully frightened, that young woman. She spoke a different language that I didn't understand but I spoke gently and said I would help her and I crouched down and helped the baby come out. His head came out alright but he needed a little help getting his shoulders to pop out but finally they did and so did he, in a hurry. What a miracle it is, a new person coming out of a person! It is the most amazing thing there is in the whole world! Better than anything else you could ever imagine! So then I helped cut his cord, and washed him off in the sink, and wrapped him up in a towel, and gave him to the young woman, who was now very embarrassed that a strange man had seen her without her clothes on. So I smiled and said thank you for such a wonderful thing as this new man in the world, and I said I would pray for him and her in my own way, and I went on. So let us think of that story the rest of today, a new person coming out of a person!

# XIII

But of course that older soldier *had* recognized me, says Cat, when he and I looked each other in the eye back there in the road, and soon I was arrested again by the soldiers.

This time I was told that I was in very serious trouble, because I would be charged not only with war crimes from the past but with kidnapping and assaulting an officer of the state, and escaping from lawful incarceration, and active flight from inquiry by officers of the state charged with the security and safety of the public. That was how the judge said the words, very momentous and careful, like they were being written in the air.

This was in his judicial chambers in a town by a small lake. Outside the window as he was talking I could see swans in the lake and

117

cranes over it. You could hear the cranes if you listened hard. They have a low croaking sound sort of like frogs, did you ever hear cranes? Cranes sound like they have had chest colds for a thousand years.

Your plea? said the judge.

I explained why I was in the country, says Cat, and I give that judge a lot of credit, he listened very carefully, with his face held in his hands like a flower in a vase.

And your lashing of the chief of the soldiers, can you explain that?

I explained that he had lashed me thoroughly first, and I apologized for having lost my temper, and explained that something had held my hand when I raised my stick there in the cave, I wasn't at all sure what it was, but I was grateful for that, because I was weary of violence, having seen enough for ten lifetimes, and no longer wished to add to the sea of bile.

The judge deliberated for a while and then the older soldier gave his testimony about how they caught me, an escaped soldier of the failed regime, a committer of war crimes, a refugee from justice as decreed by the state, and how I had in some way escaped justice, and been at large in the community, a risk and danger to the public, and had then kidnapped and assaulted and beaten an officer of the state, and again escaped, until chance, or the hand of justice, had appointed my capture again, leading to, the older soldier fervently hoped, the imposition of sentence, and imprisonment as fit crimes various.

Out on the lake at this time, says Cat, geese and ducks had also joined the swans and cranes, and I could see herons of two colors, and also egrets.

The judge deliberated for another long while, and then asked me about my childhood, and my father, and how he gave me my stick, and my sister, and how she helped me escape after the war, and The Stork, and the other men in my patrol, and how the woodworker helped make four feet for me, and about the boy who was simple, and the place in the mountains where one army nailed children's hands to trees, and then he asked me to tell him about my wife and sons at home, and what our house was like, and did we have a dog?

I explained that we used to have a dog but that the dog tried to attack a car that nearly struck my younger son and the dog died under the car, and since then my sons had birds of various colors for pets, we had four of five birds loose around the house at any one time, small friendly birds who would sit on your shoulder and sing along with the radio, which is a most remarkable sight, two or three sparrows and such singing their heads off when opera comes on the radio, ha!

The judge deliberated for another long while and then he made a pronouncement. The court recorder wrote the pronouncement down officially. Later they gave me a copy of the pronouncement to carry on my person in case of subsequent arrest and questioning by police, soldiers, and or any other agents of the state as lawfully constituted at that time. The war is over, said the pronouncement. Victory does not permit the successful general accusation of criminal activity by the other side, and no citizen of this country, past or present, who has laid aside his or her implements of violence shall be imprisoned on grounds of previous activity without proof of criminality beyond the criminality of war.

The older soldier and the judge discussed the pronouncement for quite a while after the judge issued it, says Cat, and I listened with real interest, despite the remarkable number of birds out on that lake; there was one enormous bird hovering over the lake which I thought was an eagle, but I couldn't see it very well from where I was sitting in the judicial chambers.

We are not going to have much of a country if we spend a lot of time hunting down people who were on the other side a long time ago, said the judge to the soldier, who cautiously agreed that this made sense. The fact is that our side won the war, said the judge, but that doesn't make the other side wrong, exactly. It only defines it as the losing side, and curiously then, for us, being the victor means that we have the responsibility to create a peaceful country. The price of victory by force of arms, then, is the establishment of a national entity where arms are not the arbiters of agreement. You follow.

The older soldier allowed as he did follow, says Cat, although he pointed out that being the winning side did indeed, in his opinion, not to mention his chief's, allow you to dictate what was criminal activity and what was not, and in his opinion, not to mention his chief's, armed violence during the war against members of the winning army *did* constitute criminal activity, which is why the accused eventually fled the country after the war.

I spoke up then, says Cat, and pointed out that I didn't escape because I had committed crimes, I escaped because there wasn't much of a future then for members of the losing army who had lost feet in the war, and both the judge and the soldier allowed as this was true. The soldier then registered some objections about me kidnapping the chief of soldiers and assaulting him in the cave, but the judge noted that the chief had imprisoned and assaulted me first, so that the first event ipso facto led to the second. I also pointed out that if my army had won the war, we might be in exactly the opposite positions in this room today, the older soldier and I, and this made us all stop and think for a moment.

It *was* an eagle out on the lake, says Cat, which was most remarkable, none of us had ever seen an eagle that close before, and it was an enormous and beautiful and momentous bird, with a grey head and white legs and white tail like the rudder of a boat. It was soaring over all the other birds and they flinched when its shadow went over, but none of the other birds seemed really afraid, which was interesting. We all watched it for a few moments, the soldier and the judge and the court reporter and I, and then the judge told me I was free to go, don't forget to carry a copy of the pronouncement on my person for the remainder of my travels, best wishes for safe passage and joyous return home. The soldier and I looked at each other for a moment, and then he extended his hand, and we shook hands, neither of us smiling, and then I went on.

# XIV

Today I have no answers for your questions, says Cat quietly. Today is not such a good day for talking. Some days are just like that. It's no one particular thing. No particular reason. Some days the things I have done don't seem like much to talk about. Some days I don't seem to have done so much. I don't have much money, my house is small, my family small, my sisters far away, many people I love have died, my job is exhausting. Also, hey, I have a metal foot. Did I ever show you the new foot? No? I went to the foot store, where there are hundreds of feet, feet designed for every sort of person. Whatever thing it is that you like to do, there's a foot for you. Climbing mountains, running, skiing, whatever. You can buy a foot now that has a computer in it so your foot thinks for itself, did you know that? Now there's something to think about. If your hand could think for itself, would it behave? Ha!

After I came back from looking for my foot, I stayed with rubber feet for a long time, very springy, I liked the way it felt, but one time I was at the beach with my wife and sons and we had a bonfire and I fell asleep and my foot melted! What do you think of that! So I went with wooden feet again for a while, until one day I came home from work and took off my boot and my foot fell out, you see I had broken it, coming down a ladder, but I didn't know that until it skittered across the bedroom floor, and I said come back here, foot! which may be something no one ever said before, ha!

Anyway that sent me to the foot store, and while I was amazed at the high prices, I was also amazed at the selection of feet. Things have really changed with feet in my time. I mean, it used to be that you had a choice of four of five feet, and now there are hundreds. My sons say I should get a foot with a computer in it so they can do their homework on it as I am watching television or reading but I tell them no way.

You can buy feet in different colors, says Cat. You can buy special socks for the type of foot you buy. You can buy special shoes for the feet you buy. You can buy feet that look good in sandals. You can buy feet made of wood, plastic, or metal. It's fun to go to the foot store, if you can ignore the amazing prices for a moment, just to see how creative people are when building and shaping feet. I always come home happy for some reason. You would think that you would come home sad, that you even had to go to the foot store, but as my sons say look at it this way, you didn't have to go to the elbow and hand and knee store, did you? Which is a very ood point.

But today I am weary, says Cat. Today I don't have any stories. I am out of stories. Can't find them inside. I have mislaid my stories. They'll be back tomorrow, I bet. Don't you worry. Those stories are around here somewhere. You come back tomorrow and we will call for them, come back here, you stories! Ha!

Well, there is one story I will tell you before you go, says Cat. Once a month or so the end of my leg where my new foot is, it just hurts like the devil. This happens about once a month, I think because my leg just gets tired and annoyed and cranky, like a kid does. But you can see how that could happen, that makes total sense, so I don't grudge it a bad hurt once a month or so. But the story I wanted to tell you is this: my wife rubs my leg so gently, so quietly, so steadily, without ever saying anything or complaining or making that little sigh of complaining, that I just want to cry because she is so gentle and steady. There's another feeling for which we don't have good words yet, isn't that so? She just can tell that my leg is really hurting and she just picks up my leg and takes me foot off and rubs and rubs. Boy, that is a remarkable woman. That's all I wanted to say today.

Did I ever tell you how I met my wife? says Cat. No? Well. She worked in a laundry shop, she was the girl at the counter, and one day my uncle sent me to the shop to pick up his pants, he was a fairly wealthy fellow and could afford to have his pants cleaned and pressed at a shop instead of in the basement like everybody else, so I met her, and that was pretty much that for me, and I think for her too. Anyway the immediate problem was that I didn't have any money, this was after the war when there was no work, so for a while there I couldn't figure out how to get into the shop without having any shirts or pants that needed to be cleaned and pressed, so for a while there all I did was walk past the shop every morning and evening as if I was just going to and from work, you know? And I volunteered to pick up my uncle's clothes, but he never really went anywhere, so he hardly needed his clothes cleaned and pressed, he just had it done for show, so more than once I spilled things on him not by accident, but you can only do that a couple of times without being obvious what you are doing, and I saved up what money I could and brought a shirt of my own to the shop one time, and one time I actually found a shirt by the river and brought that to the shop, but then I ran out of ideas.

I was getting pretty frazzled about this when one day as I walked past the shop in the evening, looking in the window to see her, she came out of the shop! I almost fainted! And she said to me *I like you, would you like to go get a cup of tea tonight*! Right there in the street! Can you believe it! Ha! I say that to her a lot still just to see her smile to remember, I say *I like you, would you like to have a cup of tea*

129

*tonight*? And she smiles sort of sideways, you know what I mean? She is a most remarkable woman. She doesn't think she is beautiful or smart or charming but she is the most beautiful and smart and charming woman you ever saw, partly because she doesn't *think* she is, you know? But she is. She is very funny and witty in a very gentle way. You never know what she is going to say when she opens her mouth, that is another thing about her. She says very unexpected things. She has her own way of thinking about things also. This can be very frustrating. But that is how she is. You cannot change how someone really is, that's one thing I have learned. Sometimes she decides something is so even if there is no way in the world it is so, but no one could ever convince her otherwise if that's what she decided, so you can see how this can be frustrating. But she is so gentle and funny and as you might expect she is also the greatest mother there ever was, although I think sometimes she has been too nice to our sons, I think she should have been a little harder and stricter with them, that would have been good for them, but what do I know?

Anyway we liked each other more and more

the more we had tea and finally we came to an understanding. I tease her that she got married to me only because she didn't want to drink so much tea anymore, ha! Another thing she teaches me by being her is that everyone talks about love all the time but no one knows what they are talking about. All the things you read and see in books and movies and television about love, those are only the pinkie fingers of love, you know? Real love is very complicated and needs a lot of tea, and it stretches out over time like a really long cat, you never see the whole cat at the same time. Now you got me talking about time as a cat and I have no idea what I am saying and had better stop. Ha!

So today I am weary, says Cat, today I have nothing to say, today I have no stories in my mouth. Some days are like that. Some days your heart is low and you hang your head and your feet hurt. Today is one of those days. People say it has to do with the barometer but that is silly talk. It's just that sometimes you have no gas in the tank. I think of it as a heating ventilation and cooling problem. Sometimes your valves and ducts are clogged, yes? Sometimes I think that priests and doctors and therapists and psychologists and psychiatrists and healers and shamans and monks and nuns and parents are all in the heating ventilation and cooling business, you know? Often now that my sons are getting older all I do is listen carefully and say something more carefully. They don't listen to me, exactly, but if I say the right something, gently, it sort of floats there over the kitchen table for them to poke at and think about. Mostly what they do is try to shoot it down, but sometimes they don't. I used to be annoyed when they didn't listen, but then I realized maybe I wasn't listening either. So now I just try to listen. I tease my wife that eventually I won't say anything at all ever again, and she says like *that* will ever happen! Ha!

# XV

I went on toward the southwest, says Cat, after my time with the judge and the older soldier, and I still had two little cakes in my pocket from the woman in the tea shop, and now I had the judge's pronouncement, which actually did make me feel a lot safer. Funny that a piece of paper would actually make you feel different, but there it is. This happens with driver's licenses and college diplomas and passports and report cards and birth certificates and receipts for purchase, yes? Sometime I think it is nutty that way papers get to be the kings of people, but there it is.

Anyway I went on, and now I could smell salt in the air. I was near to the ocean. I remembered that smell so vividly. We lived near the sea when I was young. You could always hear it humming in the distance. My sister used to say that the ocean wore white, a white mantle over it in the morning and a white scarf when it met the land. She called the ocean the blue lady. She used to say that the ocean was always making love to the land, ha! My mother would frown when my sister said that, as it sounded rude, but my father would smile, and say yes, sometimes love is a war. My father said a lot of mysterious things like that. He worked in a factory where he didn't say anything all day because the machines were roaring, so when he came home he liked to talk quietly and steadily for hours. There is love and not-enough-love, that's all, he liked to say. There is broken love and healthy love. It has nothing to do with good and evil. Evil is not-enough-love. He would talk to anyone, my dad. My mother used to say we had so many animals around the house because my dad needed as many ears as possible to fill. When he got really old my dad lost his voice, isn't that sad? The man who liked to talk more than anyone you ever met, he couldn't talk at all. These things happen. A remarkable man, my dad. I have a lot of stories about my dad.

Anyway I went on, down and down and

134

down out of the mountains, and it began to be sandy all around, and palm trees, and very tall ferns, and little fishing boats in people's yards, and the houses were lighter colors. It is interesting to me that houses in the mountains and forest are darker, and houses near water are lighter, why is that? is that the way it is all over the world? One of my sons says that people get lighter the less sun they see, and darker the more sun they see, that's why darker people live near the equator, so I wonder if it's like that with color and water, the closer you are to water the brighter your color. Could that be, you think?

Anyway I walked through this long flat sandy country for what seemed like a long time. One day I was in a building filled with computers of every shape and size. A remarkable place. All the workers seemed to be teenagers. I am not sure what kinds of computers they were there but they made a wonderful music when they were all working together, as did the teenagers. Another day I was at a shop where the people made wings for birds to be used in plays and theater productions. I was getting tea in a shop next door when a man came in and said do you like birds? and I said yes and he said do you want to make some money? and I said yes and he put me to work making wings—herons, owls, eagles, hawks, swans, geese, ducks, cranes, parrots, parakeets, doves, sparrows, swallows, egrets, and hummingbirds, I remember that there were fifteen kinds of birds they needed to make and the girl who had been making owls ran away from home so they were terribly behind on owls. I stayed there for three days making owl wings, can you believe it! When I got the job I have now I had to fill out papers about all the jobs I had in the past and it was a lot of fun to write down, *made owl wings*, boy, did I get questions about that, ha!

Believe it or not right after that I was walking down the street in a town and my friend the Stork walked past me! Boy, were we surprised! I recognized him right away partly because he was so tall but also because I had liked him, you know, and there's some extra kind of remembering people you like, you can pick them out in a crowd even if they are faced the other way, you can tell they are them from the way they walk, things like that. Anyway we stopped and had tea and it was just wonderful to talk. He had never married but he had a son who was also now a brand-new teacher. His son had been a soldier. He wasn't as close to his son as he wanted to be, but he figured a little close was a lot, and better a little than none. He was always a philosopher kind of person. Another thing of which he was proud was that many of his students at the school had gone up to university, and one was a professor now, and another was a minister of something in the government.

So my nefarious influence ripples into the belly of the beast, he said, that was how he talked. He made me laugh. He said he had to get going, he was on his way to a wedding, his son's old girlfriend, to whom he had become quite close, and stayed so even after they stopped loving each other.

So the ripples of affection travel on in unusual directions, he said.

We shook hands and kissed each other on the cheeks and didn't say anything about the war, although we both wanted to. I told him to come stay with me and my wife and sons if ever he traveled, and he said he would, but he and I knew that he would not. Sometimes

that is the way things are, you say one thing
even though you know another thing. I used
to dislike that when I was young but then I
grew up and learned about, what is a good
word, mercy?

# XVI

Sure there have been some tumultuous and complex times with my wife, says Cat, but I don't think those are things to talk about. Some things you don't talk about. They are things for one or two people to know. I think we make too much of honesty. Maybe adamant honesty is a form of lying, you know what I am saying? People say they will be honest about everything, but of course no one is absolutely honest about *everything*, and also insisting that everything be out in the open is maybe a way of hiding, yes? A way of saying your feelings are more important than your judgment, so that when someone is hurt by what you say, you hold up honesty like a shield. But I think that is maybe dishonest.

And there have been some hard times with

my sons. One of my sons is troubled. He has troubles of various sorts. Some troubles no one can heal. My mother was a healer, did I ever tell you that? She was adept with all sorts of medicines and songs and prayers, she knew every plant and concoction and combination of beneficial smells, and when my son was very small she tried everything she knew to dispel his troubles, but people are complicated, no two people are the same. This is something we say we know but we hardly ever really stop and think how amazing and troubling it is. Amazing because in billions of years there was never a you, and for billions of years there will never be another you, isn't that the most amazing thing? And troubling because whatever you think you learn about people, you are essentially wrong, and it doesn't apply easily to any other person, either. This is frustrating, but that's just how it is.

There are a lot of stories about my mother but she died last year and I find that I still cannot come very close to those stories without falling into a dark hole so with your permission I will wait a while to tell you those stories.

You never answered any of the questions I asked, so I wrote down some more to ask you, let me see: Why really are you asking me all these questions about my trip? Do we know each other that well really? Are you a happy man or are you borrowing my happiness when you sit here with me and hear my sons laughing and drink this tea my wife makes? How come you never say anything but just sit there and smile? Are you wise or foolish? Do you have a lot of brothers and sisters? Are they near enough to come eat at your house? Is your house open for strangers? When was the last time you gave food to someone you didn't know? Is your mother alive? If she is still alive does she live with you? Is your father alive? Is he the king of the storycatchers in your family? What was the best story he ever caught? Did he choose you to be storycatcher after him or is it just an accident? Are you the smallest brother and that's why you are the storycatcher? What hand do you use when you bless yourself? Have you ever heard God or his mother speak? Are you still living in your first religion? Do you think all animals and stars have names that we just don't know what they are? Did you ever wear a helmet? When you pray do you use words? Have you already secretly pondered names for your grandchildren? When you see a beggar in the street do you say a prayer even if you don't give him money? Did you ever punch another man hard enough to break his face or your hand? Did you ever see a bear up close? When you sing do people laugh or do they start to sing too?

You think about those questions, says Cat, smiling, and I will get us some more tea.


Did I ever tell you about the soldier in the war who lived underwater? says Cat. This was where a river opened out into the sea. He had been in the army for years and years and had seen pretty much everything you could ever see. He had been wounded in pretty much every way you could be ever be wounded. His family had all been killed or driven away by the fighting and he finally concluded to leave the planet, so he took an old submarine that had been sunk in the estuary and he fixed it up so it was watertight, and he designed a series of air tubes and ducts, and he anchored it in a secret place in the river, about half a mile upriver from the estuary. It was the most remarkable little house. There was a secret tunnel to it from a cave that had a tree growing over it. The tunnel went down under the river and came up into

142

his house. He lived there for years and years without anyone knowing about it. Finally one day the way people found out was that two boys found the cave and followed the tunnel and came up into his house when he was sitting there reading and he had a heart attack and died and they had to tell their families what happened. I think his water house is still there although I am not sure. A friend of a friend told me that story and he's a true story teller.

I'll tell you one more story today and then we better call it a day, says Cat. You ask me about cruelty, and the first thing that comes to mind, if we are talking about things that happened during the war, is the time one of the soldiers in my patrol shot two of those little rhinoceroses in the valley where we were. Of all the things I could remember, I remember that morning, isn't that strange? All the shooting we did, and the man who we shot off the top of his pecker, and the soldier who was impaled in the trap, and all the poor people in the villages who got in the way of the war, and all the children who lost their parents, and all the parents who lost their children, and all the people who starved, and all the sickness and fouled water and lost hopes, and the soldier who lived underwater, and the first thing that comes to mind is those little rhinoceroses. Well, what happened was we were walking along through the forest very early in the morning, just before dawn, when it's that wet silver color in the air, and we were exhausted, we had been in a fight almost all night and were trying to find a good place to hide, and we were lost as usual, and tempers were short, and we came into a clearing and there was a mother rhinoceros and a baby, just standing there looking at us. I remember them both chewing sideways the way they do, you know, like cows. And the guy behind me just shoots the mother, who falls over without a sound, and there's a long instant when no one moves, not us or the baby rhinoceros, and then the guy behind me shoots the baby, and it falls over without a sound also. No one said anything and we just kept walking. Funny that I would remember that. The guy didn't stop to cut their horns or anything. We just shuffled through the clearing and back into the forest and that was that. So that's what I say about cruelty in the war, two little rhinoceroses just falling over without a sound.

# XVII

Finally, says Cat, one day I came to a temple and I heard my foot calling me. It was there in a temple in a holy place with many other bones. You wouldn't believe how many bones were there. A priest was there praying for the bones.

I explained why I was there and what had happened to me in the war and he said I should stay at the temple a few days and he would pray over the matter and see what was up.

He was a very nice young man, that priest. He had been born long after the war but when he was a teenager he said he suddenly knew he was supposed to become a priest and take care of the bones. Sometimes you just know what you are supposed to do. So he and the other priests in his order repaired an old temple and people brought bones from all over the country. People brought bones to it from many miles around. There are so many bones. You think that bones are like sticks or rocks or something but they are not. They are still alive although they don't look alive. It's hard for me to explain. I don't know how that could be but that's just how it is. The priest told me it took a long time for him to get used to all the voices of all the bones. He told me there were many temples with bones in that part of the country. He thought they would never find all the bones in that country but they sure would try. That's just what you have to do, he said. Otherwise the bones just call and call. You can't just leave them on the ground. You have to find a place for them to rest. Certain things you just have to do whether they make regular sense or not, you know what I mean?

I stayed at that temple for a long time. It was a very holy place. There was a hum there in the walls and tables and chairs and benches. People came and went looking for bones. Sometimes there would be men like me looking for bones that had been theirs, though more often they were looking for the bones of friends, and women and children

146

came looking for the bones of people they loved. Sometimes a child would run right to the right bones, I saw that happen with my own eyes. One time it was a little girl who ran right to a femur and said *dad!* You don't forget something like that, I'll tell you. Sometimes people would stay there for a few days until the bones called. Sometimes they went away without finding the right bones, that happened also. Sometimes the priest would talk to you and listen to you and then he would go right to your bones. Sometimes he couldn't help the person, that happened also. He was a very nice young man, that priest. He didn't say very much. We liked each other. I told him about the simple boy I had traveled with, the boy who was up in the mountains, and about the place where people's hands had been nailed to trees in the war, and the chicken man and his motorcycle, and the place where the new religion had been born, and other stories, and he listened carefully. Very good skill, listening carefully. Highly underrated, if you ask me. sometimes I think that is the holiest skill there is. I am not such a great listener as some people, although I have tried to get better at it. One thing I have learned is that the older you get the less you know and the more you should listen, and the less you say the more you hear, and the more you hear the more you know. Or something like that. Are you listening?

Finally one day the priest brought my foot to me. The sock and shoe had been lost, he said, which he regretted, but he had prayed a good deal over these particular bones, and it had become clear to him that this was indeed my foot.

It sure looked like my foot. It was the same size as my other foot, and had the same angle to the toes. Two of the toes were missing, and tiny bone here and there were missing, but as a whole it was surprisingly whole, given what had happened and where it had been and how much it had traveled.

I stared at it with amazement, to tell you the truth. I sort of couldn't believe that it was really there in my hand. The whole moment was pretty amazing. For one thing you don't hold your foot in your hand that often, so that was interesting, and curiously the bones were warm, not cold and lifeless like you would think. Plus, I mean, there it *was*. We had both come a long way to meet each other again, and it just came over me very powerfully that my foot should stay there in the temple. It was a good place to rest. If I brought my foot home what would I do with it really, put it on the mantelpiece, or build a little shrine or something? No. It became very clear to me that it should stay here and I should go home. I had done what I had come to do, and it was time.

The priest was delighted to have my foot back in the temple. What a story this will be to tell! he said. We chose a good place for it, a shelf about waist-high so children and old people could both see it. That shelf was thick red wood, the same sort of wood that the woodworker had made my second foot from, a wood that smelled wonderful, something like cinnamon, and it seemed just the right wood for my foot to sleep on. The priest carefully chose the right bones to share the shelf with my foot, and then he said prayers for a while, and I spent a few last moments with my foot, and then I went home.

How I got all the way home is a story for another time, you must be getting tired of me talking about my travels and adventures, but I will tell you one last story, yes? When I walked into my house, after all those weeks and months, it was nighttime, and there were candles lit all over the house, in every window and on every table there was a candle, so there was gentle light everywhere. My wife was waiting in the kitchen smiling with her hands folded like she knew I was coming home that night and when she stood to kiss me she didn't say anything at all. I kissed her all over her face, every single inch, and she smelled so wonderful, like woodsmoke and salt and honey and blackberries. One of my sons was asleep and I went in and sat on the edge of his bed and woke him gently by hugging him and he hugged me like a bear for a very very long time. My other son I discovered was awake, he was upstairs in his bed and when I came in he looked up and says oh, have you been gone, papa, I didn't notice, and I fall on him in his bed and we wrestle and we laugh and cry and laugh. Ha! That boy is a teaser! He didn't *notice*! Ha!